DUPLEX DOUBLE TROUBLE

CEECEE JAMES

~For my own cute family of flamingos 333~

CONTENTS

BLURB

Duplex Double Trouble by CeeCee James

Stella's latest client is anxious to sell his half a duplex, but shortly before he's to sign the closing papers, he's murdered under mysterious circumstances.

One set of footprints that lead to the home is the only clue left behind, leaving the authorities to surmise it must've been a robbery gone wrong. They immediately set their sights on a group of petty thieves, but Stella is not so convinced they are to blame.

As she digs for answers, she uncovers a slew of possible suspects and a possible motive that may still be inside the victim's home.

Can she unravel the mystery behind his murder while trying to resist the urge to murder her own family for the secrets that continue to come to light about her past and her mysterious mother? She's just as determined to know the whole truth as they are determined to keep her from finding out.

1

The pounding on the front door jerked me straight from the bed with my hair tufting from my scalp like a Chia Pet. I had one thought, *what time is it?*

Now you'd think the time would be the last thing brewing on my mind. Given the situation, it should be much more focused on who was trying to rip down my door. I blinked, straining to see in a room pitch black from the blinds that I'd kept drawn for over a week. A sour scent filled the air, probably me, I assumed. I hadn't exactly been on point with my personal care, as the orange crumbs scattered across the bed covers from the cheese puffs that I'd nozzled the night before glaringly attested.

The knocking continued on the door, scarily insistent. I

scrambled from the bed and crept down the stairs. As stealthy as I could, I peeked around the corner.

A face peered back through the square window at the top of the door. Dark eyes narrowed at the sight of me.

So much for stealth.

I jerked out of sight and cringed. Why him? Why now? I glanced at my t-shirt, comfy, soft, and stained with spaghetti sauce. When had I eaten the spaghetti? And was that a chocolate smear? Cookie crumbs? How long had I been wearing this?

The door shook under the demanding knocks.

"Stella!" he yelled. "I know you're in there. Open up."

I couldn't ignore him. It was Officer Carlson, his bald-shaven head covered by his hat.

"C-coming!" I yelled. My voice sounded croaky and weird. It hadn't been used for a while. I ran back to my room and wiggled into my jeans. Good grief, they weren't buttoning. A week's worth of junk food acted that fast?

Desperately, I dug through the closet until I found a long sweatshirt. I yanked it over my head and tried to find a scrunchie. There were none.

The pounding on the door had become one long staccato, like

the world's worst alarm clock. Giving up, I grabbed a baseball cap and covered my hair.

I ran down the stairs, took a deep breath, and opened the door.

Carlson's tall, beefy frame filled up most of the space. His expression of professionalism dropped into a dramatic display of shock as he contemplated me. Since he was a seasoned cop who'd seen a few things in his career, I wasn't sure if I shouldn't take a little pride in rattling him.

No...no, that was hot embarrassment that I felt, not pride.

"Stella?" His hand reached toward me. It stopped short of touching my arm as if his inner voice screamed out to watch the boundaries. The warmth of his skin caressed mine as it hovered, ready to make contact should I give him any inclination it was okay. "No one has seen or heard from you in almost two weeks. Are you okay?"

Ahhh, that's why my jeans won't button. I tried to nod, unable to meet his eyes, desperately needing to get him off my porch and out of there before that mental wall I had inside came tumbling down. I couldn't be open with him—anyone—about the pain and betrayal raging inside my soul right now. *Please go away, please go.*

"Stella." His voice was lower, firmer, drawing my eyes

upward. His own were soft, full of concern. "I can tell you're not okay."

I tried to rally one more time, to scrape up that last bit of strength to resist breaking down. My bottom lip trembled. Who was I kidding? I was about as emotionally stable as a pile of sand, swept under by the slightest breeze of kindness.

At my reaction, he stepped through the doorway and was next to my side. His hand was gentle as he grasped my arm. "What's going on?"

I shook my head, the words caught in my throat in a vise of pain.

Slowly, his hand trailed up to my shoulder and squeezed. "Take your time," he encouraged. "Deep breaths."

I ducked my head again, hiding under the brim of the hat. "I just got some bad news about my mom."

His voice dropped more, tinged with dread. "Is she okay?"

Realizing how that sounded, I quickly nodded. But was she really? My nod faded into a shrug. "It's not like that. I haven't seen her since I was a little girl. She's been a kind of dark secret all my life. Last week, my Uncle Chris told me more about her—not good news—and I'm trying to process." I couldn't tell him more. I wasn't ready.

His thumb stroked my shoulder a few times and then his

hand dropped to his side. I was surprised he didn't press for more answers.

"Well, I can tell you that there are people in your corner who care about you." He cleared his throat. "Your—uh—your father was quite concerned at not hearing from you. He asked us to make a welfare check."

Hearing about my father snapped that inner wall back up nice and firm. Anything about my father would right now. The wall was built by anger in the first place.

Carlson seemed to sense the change in me and changed the subject to a new topic. "So, what are you doing around here? Flooring?" He pointed to the new laminate that was half-laid, the task forgotten as the full boxes stacked against the wall proved.

I nodded, barely able to respond as the anger built. In fact, I was mentally counting to ten to combat the offense that my father would intrude on me in this way. Call the police? This was all *his* fault to begin with.

"Good job. I'm impressed." He winked at me, and then said more seriously, "If you need me, Hollywood, text me. I'll be here."

Hearing the nickname he persisted in using since we first met did make me smile, albeit grudgingly. "Thank you, Carlson," I said.

He tipped his hat. "Name's actually Ethan. No one has called me that in years. I've never liked it."

"Ethan?" I wrinkled my nose.

"Hey, you told me your secret, so I told you mine. But you call me Ethan out there," he jerked a thumb outside, "and I might have to put you under arrest."

"Ooooh," I said, smiling now for real.

"Yeah, well maybe not. You might like that too much." He grinned, flashing strong white teeth. "I'll see you around, Hollywood." He stepped off the porch, his great height making the boards shake.

"Take care, E.... Carlson," I changed as he turned back with his index finger up and a warning look.

He nodded with approval. As he approached his car, I could hear him whistling.

Even though I wasn't smiling as I shut the door, I felt better. Maybe it was time to deal with the internal knot of emotions rather than stay on this self-destructive path of pizza deliveries and ice-cream.

As Carlson backed out, my phone vibrated with a call. Sometime last week I'd stuffed it under the couch cushion, so I was surprised there was any juice left to allow it to ring.

Lifting the cushion, I fished it out.

Not surprisingly, it was Dad. Carlson must have just called in the all clear. Feeling slightly betrayed by the cop, I pushed accept.

"Stella." The relief in my father's voice was palatable.

"I'm fine. I just need some time," I said, cutting to the chase.

"I know what's going on. Your uncle called me."

Of course, Uncle Chris called him. Those two had conspired to keep this secret about my mom away from me for my whole life. Just the thought of their colluding together made my blood boil.

I couldn't keep it in any longer and my thoughts tumbled out in angry words. "Why would you keep me from my mom? Why didn't you try to maintain a relationship with her? What's the story between the two of you?"

His voice tightened, and his words came out like his throat felt raw. "Why don't you ask your dear grandfather about that."

He'd brought up Oscar, which hit me like a kick in the gut. "Dad, you aren't taking responsibility. This isn't about Oscar. This is about you and your decision. I just can't do this right now." I blew out a big breath. "I need some space. I'll talk to you later."

"Stella, please..."

As angry as I was, I hated hearing the pain he was feeling. "Just give me some time. I have to figure this out." With that, we hung up.

The phone call acted like an anchor, doing its best to drag me back down to the dark place. I caught a glimpse of myself in the hall mirror, crazy hair peeking out from under the hat, purple circles under my eyes, a dirty shirt. My gaze fell to the table underneath covered in a pile of unsorted bills, then I glanced back at the unfinished flooring I'd promised my landlady I'd put in.

I was about to lose it all, with no money coming in.

Was I going to let them do this to me again?

"No!" I said out loud. I shook my head and walked over to the mirror, jabbing my index finger at my reflection. "Stella O'Neil. You are stronger than this. You can't change the past, only the future. Get your butt into gear. Pull yourself out of this swamp and get back to living life."

My stern face stared back at me. Giving myself an approving nod, I ran upstairs to the shower. I was getting my power back.

Little did I know what was coming down the road to try and shake it.

2

*A*bout an hour later, I arrived at the Flamingo realty. My Uncle Chris owned the business, and the promise of reuniting with my family, as well as an adventure, was one of the reasons I'd relocated to Pennsylvania from Seattle. But after the horrid conversation with Uncle Chris— where he revealed that my mother had not abandoned me as a little girl, but that she'd been in prison all these years, not to mention she'd been arrested by my grandfather in a drug sting —I'd obviously been avoiding coming into work. I still wasn't ready to come back, but I had to make some money or I was going to lose the little cottage I'd grown to love.

As far as seeing Uncle Chris again, well I wasn't sure what I was going to say to him. I guess I'd cross that bridge when I came to it.

I got out of the car and surveyed the building, taking in its pink flamingo motif painted on the front window. I thrust on a pair of sunglasses and pushed my shoulders back, then strode into the office with my head high.

The building was cool and dim in comparison to the bright outdoor light of today's warm spring day. My eyes immediately were drawn to Uncle Chris's office in the back. His door was shut. You'd think that would have brought some relief, but it didn't. I wasn't sure if delaying the inevitable was a good thing or not.

"Stella!" Kari called, her voice filled with excitement.

Seeing her sweet face made my resolve stutter. My co-worker, and my first friend in town. There's something about meeting a friend for the first time after something really horrible happens that makes all that pain bubble to the surface again.

Tears stung my eyes, and I blinked them back.

Oh, no! Her face was softening in a very sympathetic expression. She got up from her desk and started walking over. I pressed my lips together. *Be strong! Don't cry!*

"Aw, Stella. You okay?" she asked, her forehead wrinkling in concern.

Those were the exact words that would ensure I would not be

okay. I shook my head as a lump grew in my throat too big to talk over.

"Girlie." She sighed and slung her arm around my shoulders to hug me. Every muscle shook as I forced myself to breathe deep and to not break down.

"Your uncle said you were having a rough time. He told me a little bit about what was going on. He shouldn't have, you know. It's just that he feels terrible and it spilled out."

I pulled away, nodding, and wiped at my eyes. "Yeah. Things are messed up right now."

"Look at the good side, you found out your mom is alive. And now you know she didn't just leave...." Kari let the last thought drop without completing it.

It had already been a rough morning. "I can't think about it right now." I tried to smile. "I'm back because I have to be."

"Okay. Well I have the perfect distraction." She snapped her fingers and changed gears briskly. "How about a house showing! A couple of potential buyers found one of our listings on the internet and want to see it. You can take them."

"You want me to show your client's house?" I asked, a little skeptically.

"Of course! Good for me because I've been feeling kind of

funky and can get some of this paperwork done. Good for you so that you can be distracted. Truth be told, once I saw your car pull up, I immediately sent them a text letting them know my assistant would be there." She paused with a small smile. "To sweeten the pot, think of the split commission if you're able to sell it. I know things must be pretty tight for you."

"Aw, Kari, I can't let you do that for me."

"Nonsense. That's what friends are for. Besides, Joe just locked down a new job so we're doing fine. Now about the showing, the owner's name is Charlie Booker. Don't get your hopes up, though. This one's been tricky. For one thing, there's his sister who lives with him. I don't think she wants Charlie to sell the place. The last time I showed it, I swear she'd sabotaged it by leaving the place a disaster. And then there's the neighbor. They're also making it a challenge to get this puppy sold."

Gratefulness filled me from Kari's kindness. I cleared my throat and tried to get into the professional groove. "Thank you, Kari. I appreciate it. Now, what's the neighbor doing?"

"Oh, you'll see when you get there." She hurried back to her desk and grabbed something from a plastic container. "Here, to fortify you."

It was a homemade blueberry muffin. Well, now, I guess I

could use some fortification. I peeled off the wrapper and took a bite before taking out my little purple spiral from my purse. I opened to the first page and froze, seeing my mother's name and the year she was arrested inked in dark letters with sad crying faces. Quickly, I turned to a blank page just as Kari rattled off the MLS number and address. I jotted it down, along with the names of both the clients and the owner. With her cheering me on like I was part of a high school basketball team, I headed out to meet my distraction.

As I PULLED up to the duplex, I saw for myself that Kari wasn't exaggerating about the neighbors. The neighbor's side had plastic fish plastered down the wall like they were caught in a waterfall. Gnomes decorated the grass, along with fake mushrooms and eclectic plastic woodland creatures. Of course, maybe they weren't so out of place, after all, what with our giant pink flamingo for-sale sign in front of Charlie Booker's side.

It had rained hard at some point during the night, and there were muddy tire prints in the edge of the lawn from where a car had veered off while backing out. I assumed it was the owner of the duplex since another car was sitting at the entry of the driveway.

The car held a youngish couple that got out as I parked. I grabbed my notebook. There was no time to double-check how I looked, not with the buyers already walking towards me. I only hoped the blueberry muffin hadn't left a friend in my teeth.

The fresh scent of spring wrapped around me as I climbed out. I couldn't even help the deep breath I took in, as if my lungs were greedy after being cooped up in a stale house for over a week.

It felt like a lot of things had changed in the world since I'd last been out, as the petite leaf buds on the bushes and daffodil's poking their heads up along the brick-edged flowerbed attested. The duplex was tucked in nearly by itself, hidden among a lot of farmland. There were a couple of houses across the street and a driveway I'd passed on my way in, but otherwise, the neighborhood was acres of grass with a long line of those leafy water-loving trees running behind the fields. I suspected there was a creek or river someplace in the middle of those trees.

At the crunching footsteps, I turned to face the approaching couple.

"Are you with Flamingo Realty?" asked the man.

"Hi, there," I said in my 'your friendly neighborhood real estate agent' voice. It was like riding a bike. I walked over with my hand extended. "I sure am. Stella O'Neil, and I do represent the seller. And you must be..."

A guy in his forties took my hand and shook it. Not as young as I'd first thought. There was a woman with him, younger, with her hair pulled up in a sloppy bun.

"Gary Davis. Nice to meet you. My friend here decided to tag along to give her opinion." He jerked his thumb in the direction of the woman next to him.

"Hi, friend," I said, my hand out.

She laughed. "Tina. He needs someone to ground him because he's such a dreamer. I call him a Peter-Panner."

"A dreamer, huh?" I asked.

"Everyone should be," Gary answered, unabashed. "Speaking of dreams...." His gaze swept over the neighbor's decorations. "That collection could give someone nightmares."

"Yes, well." I bit my lip, embarrassed. I wasn't quite sure how to verbally navigate around such an obvious eye-sore.

"Nah, It's not a big deal for me. My grandparents have tons of those. Reminds me of home." He gave an easy-going grin.

Nice!

Together, the four of us walked to the front door. It was red and appeared to have been recently painted. I knocked hard to be sure the owners had left. When there was no answer, I went for the key box.

A click and the turn of the knob and we were inside. The interior of the home appeared fairly typical for today's modern duplexes. There was a long great room with a kitchen that ran into a dining area at one end. Luckily, it seemed to be free of any sabotage that Kari had said Charlie's sister had done earlier.

Gary walked down the narrow hall. There were four doors, the first opening to reveal an office.

"Kind of messy," Gary noted.

That was an understatement. The room was dark as the window had its curtains closed. There was an enormous bookshelf against one wall and a stack of boxes leaning near the other. They weren't packing boxes, meant to help the owner move. Instead, they were of all shapes and sizes, like Charlie Booker was a big online shopper. I made a mental note to suggest the owner move them if this showing didn't pan out. They were way too distracting.

Gary turned around. "I'm a little surprised. This room seems really small." He jammed his hands into his pockets as his brow puckered in disappointment.

"I think this area would appear bigger without the boxes." I briskly walked over to the blackout curtains and heaved them to the side. Sunlight streamed in.

"Wow! Just look at the view!" Gary exclaimed.

From here you could see how the grassy field lay like a flowing carpet before the blue mountains in the distance.

"That's amazing! Why would they keep those shut?" asked Tina.

I shrugged. People did questionable things, as I'd discovered soon after starting in this business.

"Who knows?" I answered. "But can't you just imagine what an amazing office this would be?"

Gary's eyes grew introspective as he walked over to the window. He stared outside for a moment and then spun around. "I could put my distillery here."

"Oh, Gary." Tina rolled her eyes.

"What? I'm serious." He scowled.

"You could do whatever your heart pleases." I nodded in agreement. "You want to check the rest of the house?"

"Neighbor seems quiet," Gary murmured.

As he said that, barking could be heard, the kind that came from a little dog. And then a woman yelled, "Shush!"

"Spoken too soon," laughed Tina.

"Naw, that doesn't bother me. I like animals."

Gary. Gary. So easy to please. I liked him.

We walked down the hall to the next room, which was surprisingly much bigger. The master bedroom had the expected en suite which led to Tina admiring the bathroom with its soaking tub and walk-in closet. I noticed Gary had disappeared and quickly tracked him down to find him in the living room, staring slack-jawed in front of the largest big-screen TV I'd ever seen.

"I think I'm in love. Does this come with the house?" he asked.

I assumed he was joking, yet played along. "You never know. Everything's negotiable."

He found the remote on the coffee table and flipped on the TV.

"Oh, my goodness," Tina murmured, her eyes going wide.

I glanced over at the screen, and a thrill of shock zipped through me. That was me, right there in the middle one of the six split squares on the television screen. I waved, and my image waved back at me. I turned around, scanning for the camera.

"He's got some hefty security system," Gary said as he clicked it off. "Make sure to include the TV and the security system if I decide to make an offer."

I still couldn't find any of the cameras. Was it one of those ultra secret weird ones in electric sockets? I'd seen that on one of my detective shows. I pulled out my purple notebook and pen from my purse and scribbled his request.

"You got it," I confirmed.

Gary strolled over to the sliding glass door. He flipped the lock and stepped out onto the screened patio.

Despite being a duplex, both yards were fully fenced with six-foot plank. There was a hot tub out in the yard and a wet bar, along with a barbecue and a few lounge chairs. Gary walked over to the tub and lifted the insulation corner to peer inside. As I watched, he started playing around with the control pad.

With a heavy sigh and slow steps, Tina moved into the kitchen and turned on the sink's faucets. She hummed as she shut it off and then leaned against the counter to stare out the window.

I set down the notebook and joined her.

"Seems like he likes it," she said, her lip curling up in amusement.

As if he could hear us, Gary glanced at the window. Feeling caught, I backed away, bumping into Tina who was doing the same.

"We probably looked like two owls watching him," I muttered, shaking my head.

She laughed. She was a cute girl and it made me wonder if Gary wished they were more than friends.

A moment later the slider opened. Gary walked in with a grin which he quickly dropped when he saw me. Please. He couldn't fool me. I knew a bluff when I saw one.

"Great yard, right?" I asked.

"Yeah." He cleared his throat. "It will do."

I glanced at my watch. We'd used up all the allotted time I'd reserved for the showing, and then some. Still, as far as I was concerned, if staying meant they'd buy the house, then we'd wait until the cows came home.

It wasn't going to be needed though. I was confident I'd be hearing from Gary soon. "You guys ready to go?" I slipped behind him and locked the slider.

He nodded. "Yeah. Thanks for meeting us out here. It's a nice place."

We walked to the front door, and I held it open for them.

"Don't wait too long. Despite the gnomes, the market is hopping. So, if you like it, I'd jump on it right now."

He glanced at Tina. "What do you think?"

"I think we need a few minutes to talk."

His nose wrinkled like he didn't want to hear that, but he seemed to respect her enough to follow her advice. Turning to me, he said. "Give us some time, and I'll get back to you."

"You've got my number," I said, locking the door.

We walked to our cars. Gary turned and studied the house again. For some reason, I did the same.

Okay. That was strange. Something about the duplex brought a little niggle of premonition, a mental itch that something wasn't right. It was the same unrestful feeling when I forgot to unplug my curling iron or turn off the oven. Something about the windows…I gazed at the house, but nothing came to me.

I shook my head. Maybe that was it. Perhaps I *had* forgotten to turn something off at home.

But with all of my shut-in behavior, I definitely hadn't used my stove or my curling iron for the better part of a week. The only thing that could be left on was the microwave, the TV, and a can of spray cheese.

"See you later, Stella!" Gary called, pulling me from my musing. I waved at them and climbed into my car. Whatever was bothering me, I'm sure it would turn out to be nothing. That's how it usually worked. In the meantime, another hunch was hitting me. I needed to figure out how to write an offer that included the TV and that crazy surveillance system.

3

*I*t turned out my gut instinct was right. Gary Davis called just as I pulled in front of the Flamingo realty. I started the paperwork for his offer right away as he drove over to meet me.

He had one small caveat he wanted to include in the contract. Not only did Gary want the TV and surveillance equipment, he also wanted a twenty-four-hour expiration on his offer. The housing market was competitive enough that he didn't want to be tied up too long waiting on the seller's consideration, only to be denied.

I understood it. The terms were good. I felt confident the seller, Charlie Booker, would accept it.

I called Charlie, who answered on the third ring. "Hello?"

"Mr. Booker this is Stella O'Neil, with the Flamingo Realty. I showed your place this morning? Good news. We have an offer that I'm sure you'll love. Can I swing by to go over it with you?"

"Really? Excellent news. Is it full price?"

"It is, with a few small stipulations. Maybe I can help you find a new house as well. Do you have any ideas of where you want to move?"

"I'm not sure I want to settle down, which is causing a ruckus with my sister." He chuckled softly. "Now she has to find a new place to stay so she's not too happy with me. But I've just come into some money and I'm ready to travel. Maybe I'll settle someplace overseas. Listen, I have some things to tie up, but I can meet you at three. Would that work?"

"Sounds great!"

It was nice to hear how excited he was. Excitement flickered through me as well. Not only had I sold a house, I'd managed to not think about my mom for hours.

⁂

AT THREE O'CLOCK on the dot, with the ink on Gary's signature practically still wet on the offer, I parked at the entrance of the duplex's driveway. This time, there was a car parked in front of the garage. I assumed it was Charlie's.

The ground was still sloppy with mud. I grimaced as I picked my way through the puddles until I made it to the cracked walkway. I passed a muddy pair of footprints heading the same direction as myself. Were those from doing the showing earlier? I shook my head. Nope. Those tracks were from a pair of jogging shoes. I recognized the pattern since I'd just purchased a pair myself. The muddy prints slowly faded as they headed closer to the house, leaving only one partial impression on the first step.

Feeling like I was following a trail of bread crumbs, I mirrored the prints until I too was standing on the front porch. Shifting the contract in my hand, I knocked on the door.

The wind whistled through the trees behind the property. I took a deep breath and straightened my back. Did I bring a pen? I frowned. Surely he had one.

There was no answer.

I checked my watch. Only a minute after three. I wasn't late, and for something so important, he wouldn't have left anyway.

This time I knocked with extra gusto.

Seconds ticked by. Still no answer.

Odd. Very odd.

I stepped off the porch and observed the house for a moment. There was a twitch of a curtain, but unfortunately not from the side of the townhome I needed it to be from. It came from the neighbor's.

A face peered from the crack, along with a glimmer on the hand. A large wedding ring. I smiled and waved. The curtain immediately dropped.

I had only a second to wonder about that when the neighbor's front door opened.

"You need something?" asked a man. I couldn't gauge his age. He appeared exhausted, with bags under his eyes and drawn, gray skin.

"Yeah. I'm supposed to be meeting your neighbor. Do you know where he is?"

"Charlie's a recluse," the man said. He pursed his lips. "Check back later. Maybe his sister will be back."

"That's right. I heard she lived with him."

He shook his head. "More like mooching off of him. These walls are like paper and they fight something terrible all the time. I can hear everything. Yet, he won't kick her out."

I wasn't going to touch that with a ten-foot-pole. "Where is she, now? Do you know?"

He shrugged. "Went out jogging."

Huh. Was that the reason behind the jogging prints I saw?

Just then, a blonde woman with a mop of curly hair popped in nearly under the neighbor's armpit. He glanced down with a scowl.

The woman barked out, "When you see him, you tell him he can't have people barging in and out of his house at all hours of the night. And now he's trying to sell it? More people coming and going. It's an outrage!"

"Oh, hush, Marge," said the man gruffly.

My spine straightened at his tone. The woman glanced down and backed away. Without another look, the man shut the door.

Pleasant people. I shook my head and walked back to Charlie's side of the driveway. I wanted to look at those shoe prints again. His sister jogged, huh? That warmed my heart with a slightly kindred feeling since I jogged as well.

The frown crept over my face as I studied the muddy print. Either the sister was super tall, or she had the biggest feet I'd ever seen. Carefully, I stepped next to the one full print and noted it was quite a bit bigger than mine. It did have the

27

corkscrew sole mark though, confirming it was the brand I thought.

Interesting. It had to be Charlie's. It was odd that the shoe prints went into the house, rather than leaving it, yet no one was home. Maybe Charlie was asleep. Should I try again?

The offer in my hand rattled with the breeze. Yes, I had to get hold of him. I knocked even harder this time, only to heave a sigh when there was no answer. I slid my phone from my pocket and proceeded to give him a call.

An answering machine picked up with a message that the voice mailbox was full. Lovely. I had less than twenty-four hours to track him down before the offer expired.

Scanning the road, I walked back to the car. I had an irrational hope that I'd see his sister jogging back, but it wasn't to be. Should I wait for her?

Heck, no. If she was like me, she might be at the gym, rather than jog the neighborhood. Who knows, she could have plans to be away for the rest of the day.

It was unbelievable to be in this situation since I'd just talked with him. Charlie knew the clock was ticking.

Frustrated, I jumped back in the car to return to the office. It was out of my hands. There wasn't anything I could do now but wait.

THE NEXT HOUR dragged on at the office, with my multiple phone calls hitting Charlie Booker's full answering service. I had three phone calls from Gary Davis wanting to know where we stood with the offer. It had been disheartening to have to repeatedly tell him I was still trying to track down the seller.

The only good thing was that Uncle Chris seemed to have left for the day so I wouldn't have to worry about running into him.

"Still can't get hold of Charlie?" Kari asked. She'd been so quietly working that I'd forgotten she was even there.

I shook my head. Kari burped and covered her mouth. Her expression wrinkled with concern, and I wondered if I oughtn't to run the trash can over in case she was about to vomit.

"You okay?" I asked.

She didn't answer for a second, and then slowly nodded. "Yeah. Lunch must not have agreed with me."

"What did you have?"

"Carrots with ketchup."

My eyes bugged at the thought. "That's a weird combo." I actually meant gross, but I was going for kindness.

"Sometimes weird is where it's at. Now, since I have you here, do you have any plans for this weekend?"

I stiffened. The last time she'd asked me that was to set me up on a blind date. "Why?"

"Nothing. I just thought, with you being cooped up in your house, you might enjoy a break. Joe and I are going to try that new Mexican restaurant and wanted to know if you'd want to come."

Definitely suspicious. "Just the three of us?"

"Of course!" She smiled disarmingly. "Although there's a chance that Joe's work buddy—"

"Busy. I'm super busy." I grabbed my purse and the contract. "Listen, I'm heading out. I'll try Charlie's one more time and let you know if I find him."

She tried to play it cool, but by her facial features, you'd think disappointment was her middle name. "I will. And if you change your mind...."

"Gotta go!" I darted out of the office.

Kari. Would she ever give up? Especially after the last man she'd set me up with had started to gasp and begged me to pass him his inhaler. When I freaked out, frantically searching for it, he'd laughed and said he needed it because I took his breath away. And that was his best pick-up line for the evening, out of a seemingly plethora of them.

My mind went back to Charlie Booker. Why wasn't he answering? Was it possible that his phone was off or dead? I was super tired, the type of exhaustion that comes from spending a week holed up in a dark house with only anxiety and junk food to keep you fueled. I drove past a coffee stand and thought briefly about stopping for a drink to perk myself up.

I decided against it, not wanting anything to stop me from falling asleep tonight. My head was already full of all the things that had happened today. From Carlson showing up this morning, to getting this sale, to now having to track Charlie Booker down. It was quite an extreme from grieving over my mom just this morning.

Was I okay with things sliding back into normalcy? Putting everything I'd learned about my mom on lockdown? Or was I willing to entertain the idea of trying to find her?

I wasn't sure. Safety told me no. After all, hadn't I always kept everything about her locked away? A little prison for memories of mom....

All of those tangled thoughts evaporated the moment I

turned down Charlie Booker's road. Emergency red-and-white lights flashed from a brigade of vehicles in front of his house.

Standing across the road was a clot of people—neighbors most likely—each wearing different degrees of curiousness. None of them seemed particularly concerned beyond the normal nosiness of neighborhood gossip.

That wasn't me, however. I cared. My jaw hung slackly in my complete panic at what the lights possibly meant, and I only just missed coasting into the ditch. Luckily, I saw it in time to slam on the brakes.

I climbed out of the car in a cloud of surrealness. What on earth was going on? All of the police officers seemed busy so I walked over to the neighbors. One of them had a dog on a leash who promptly gave me a proper doggy sniff.

"What's happening?" I asked, petting the dog.

"The guy who lives in there just died," said the dog's owner. The dog twisted his leash around the woman's legs. She turned, trying to untangle herself, her forehead rumpled in frustration. "Bruno, sit!"

My legs suddenly felt like gelatin, and I nearly followed her command to her dog. "You're kidding me?"

"No." She stopped in mid-spin and nodded toward the

ambulance. "I heard one of the paramedics talking about it. Said the guy's throat was slit. Soon as they saw me watching they shut their traps. They should be more open with us. Seriously! What if that murderer is still running loose in the neighborhood? I'm home by myself, with Jerry out on long-haul."

She was peppering me with information, and none of the details were helping me get my mouth closed. I'm sure I looked like a baby bird waiting for a worm. Charlie... dead! Murdered even!

"That's his sister right over there. Maribel. She's the one who found him." The woman pointed.

My mouth gapped even further and not just because the man had died. In Maribel's hand was my purple notebook.

4

My spiral notebook! How did Charlie Booker's sister get it? The memory replayed of me bringing it into the house and jotting Gary's requests inside it as I gave the tour. I must have set it down somewhere.

Maribel tossed her brown curly hair over her shoulder and continued to talk at a speed that seemed to flummox the officer. His hands wavered in the air as if to try and calm her. Her lips curved sullenly as her grip tightened on the notebook like she was thinking about using it for a weapon.

He's going to take that away from her! Fear ignited my steps. I started down the driveway when a hand clamped hard on my arm. I swiveled to see another officer who wore a rather grouchy expression himself.

"Where are you going?" he asked. "You can't cross the tape." He was a hairy guy, with tufts poking out of his ears and a curly mat sprouting along the backs of his hands, along with a very dark five o'clock shadow.

"That woman there." I pointed. "She has something of mine. That notebook she's holding belongs to me."

He turned to follow my finger, his own eyes narrowing. Maribel seemed even more enraged, and the face of the officer she was speaking with was stiffening into a no-nonsense expression. As I watched, his hand slipped behind to where he kept his handcuffs.

"I'll check into it," said the officer in front of me.

"Check into it? She looks like she's about to get arrested. Can't you grab it for me? I left it at their house when I showed it earlier."

"Showed it?" he asked, zeroing back in on me. He reached into his belt pocket and pulled out his own pad of paper.

I sighed. *Great. Just great.* "Yes. I showed the duplex to a man who later wrote up an offer. I called Charlie Booker earlier, and we were supposed to meet at three."

"What's your name and what happened at three?"

"My name is Stella O'Neil, of Flamingo Realty. See?" I pointed to the for-sale sign. The flamingo sadly had been knocked sideways and sat, beak-up, toward the sky. "As for as our meeting, Charlie never answered. In fact, no one was home. The neighbor said the sister who lived with him had gone jogging." I lifted my chin in the direction of the brunette.

"You see anything out of place when you came by?"

I widened my eyes and shook my head, trying to appear like an innocent bystander. I didn't want to go down to the station to get fingerprinted. Again.

He exhaled, his nostrils flaring as he scribbled for a minute. Then he asked for my phone number which he added to his notes before tucking them all away. "Regarding your notebook, well, she's being interviewed right now," he explained. "You're just going to have to wait. Back here." With that, he nudged me until I was behind the start of the driveway.

I stood to the side and watched, my arms crossed. Annoyed.

Red-faced, Maribel gestured at the officer with my book, stopping just short of tapping it against his chest. His eyebrows zoomed up, and he snapped back. His words finally seemed to make her put an effort into calming down. Her hands squeezed, her eyes rolled—it was like watching an equestrian try and rein in a run-away horse. A second later, she stomped around the house.

36

"Hey!" I yelled, starting after her again.

The same hairy officer stopped me again. "What did I just tell you? You can't cross the line."

I pointed indignantly. "Look over there! You said you were going to check into my notebook. She took off behind the house!"

He glanced in that direction, before cautioning me, "I'll take care of it. You stay here, or it might be you whose under arrest."

I tried to heed his warning, but I needed that book back. It had my mother's name in it, along with private notes I'd scrawled right after I'd talked with Uncle Chris. I didn't even remember what all I'd written in that emotional heat. And there was a poem, one that would make me blush with its horrendous rhyming and sappiness. It focused on the last time I'd seen her as I finally opened my heart up about my feelings. I couldn't lose it.

Officer Grumpy-and-Hairy walked over to the cop who'd been interviewing Maribel. They talked together for a moment, and then both glanced in my direction. Officer G-and-H rolled his eyes and started around the side of the duplex in the direction the woman had disappeared.

Well, good. At least something was being done.

At that moment, a weird wailing noise tore through the air. It was coming from the woods behind the duplex. Chills ran down my arm. I glanced at the cops, but they didn't seem to notice. What was that? A ghost? Some injured hyena?

I didn't have time to ask because the hairy cop popped up on the other side of the duplex. He looked over at me and shrugged, his hands spread in a display of helplessness.

"She's taken off," he yelled.

Well, that's just great. Taken off and with my notebook. How could they let that happen?

I watched in case he had more information, but it was obvious that was all I was going to get. Officer Hairy joined the other cops, making it crystal clear that he was dismissing me from his list of troubles.

Furious, I stormed back to my car, my feet slipping on the mucky mud on the side of the road. It was then I saw a blue dog collar hidden on the other side of a row of dense bushes. A sparkle from its silver clasp had caught my eye. I picked it up, its dog tags rattling together. There was a brown stain on one side.

I ran my thumb over the metal to clear the mud. My hope was to find an address but instead there was just a name. Nymph.

What an odd choice for a dog. Of course, I didn't own a dog, in fact I'd never had a dog—Dad had been allergic—still it seemed to me that you'd want something snappy for a dog. Something you could call quickly while the dog was running away.

Then again, what did I know? Maybe someone thought Nymph was a cozy name. The collar was tiny so the moniker fit.

I walked back to the crowd by the mailboxes. It was already smaller as people dispersed. Luckily, there were still a few hanger-on's waiting for news.

"Hey, did one of you or your neighbor's lose their dog?" I held up the collar. "He's called Nymph."

The women looked at each other. One held out a hand to examine the tags, and I passed it over. Her mouth soundlessly moved as she read it and then she shook her head. "Not me. Do you know of anyone, Debbie?"

Her companion shook her head. "Maybe try the blue house up the road. I know they have a few dogs." She snorted, and I wondered about that.

I took the collar back. "Okay, thanks."

As I walked back to my car, I heard it again. That weird howling noise someplace out in the trees. What the heck was it? I glanced back at the women. They didn't seemed bothered by it. Okay then, I'd chalk it up to some type of Pennsylvania weird wildlife I knew nothing about.

I climbed in the car and tossed the collar on the passenger seat.

The ambulance passed me, sirens and lights off. Carefully, I turned the car around and ended up following it down the street. Was Charlie in the back of that ambulance? I grimaced at the thought.

It turned out that finding the driveway to the blue house was a challenge, and not just because of my distraction by the emergency vehicle. The dirt entrance ended up being buried between two overgrown hedges, so wild and intertwined they haphazardly created a tunnel. The driveway was bumpy and unwelcoming, and when I got to the end, I wasn't at all sure if I should get out. The dark windows seemed to angrily glare at me with their crooked eyebrow shutters. Nothing about the place said, "Welcome."

The decision was made for me as the door sprang open, bouncing back on rusty hinges. A man with a shotgun stepped onto a porch, whose wooden steps listed to one side.

I shrank behind the wheel. My brain screamed, "Reverse! Reverse!" Before I could reach for the gear shift, the air split with the sounds of a pack of barking dogs.

"Quiet!" the man yelled behind him. "You need something?"

he asked, his eyebrows doing a good job mimicking those broken shutters. Crowding behind him were four or five dogs, each vying for a spot to get a good look at me.

I was so gobsmacked by the sight of the rifle, I didn't respond for a second. Finally, I unrolled my window.

"Uh, I found this dog collar. The neighbors told me it might be yours." I held it out and willed my hand not to shake. The darn dog tags betrayed me with a slight rattle.

He lowered the gun. "Ain't mine. My animals don't wear collars. I think it's cruel."

"Cruel?" I asked. I chucked the collar on the dashboard.

"Yeah. How would you like to wear something tight around your neck every day."

I considered my necklace, scarves, men's ties, and thought it might be a small price to pay to make sure the animal could be identified. The way he gripped the rifle made me think it was best not to argue. All I cared about now was to get my tuchus safely back to the road.

"Okay, thank you," I said, then cringed. Why was I thanking *him*?

That seemed to alert him to the gun in his hands. He pointed it to the ground. "Sorry about that. There's been strange things going on around here. Can't be too careful."

41

"Strange like what?" I asked, forcing my hand to stop from where it was sliding the gear shifter into reverse like it had a mind of its own. "You mean the emergency situation up the road?" I pointed in the duplex's direction.

"Nah. Strange like people running through the field back there in the middle of the night. I've been leaving the dogs out to make sure no one tries any funny business with my place."

"What's back there?" I asked. "I mean, besides the field."

"Nothing but a creek. Not even good fishing. No, someone's up to trouble. Probably them teenagers out to do a little—" Here he pantomimed smoking a pipe.

"Have you ever had a good look at them?"

"Nah. They usually stay far enough back so I can't see them. They've heard me chamber ol' Deadeye here." He patted his shotgun. "Reckon they know not to come within range."

"You'd shoot them?" I said. My foot eased off the brake pedal.

"Salt-peter, and heck yes, I would. You don't mess with me or mine out here. I've got the right to defend myself."

I nodded. "Just so I'm clear, you don't know anyone with a dog by the name of Nymph in the neighborhood?"

He shook his head. "No."

"Do you see people walk their dogs often around here?"

"Yeah, occasionally. They like to slow by my driveway and try to look at my house. Get my dogs all riled up every time. Don't clean up after themselves, neither."

I was starting to wonder if this guy wasn't acting a little paranoid. "Have you seen a small dog, specifically, or know the breeds?"

Again, he shook his head.

"Okay. Well, thank you for your time." I waved and then peeked over my shoulder and backed out. He watched until I was off his driveway, then disappeared back into his house.

Once on the road, I checked down at Charlie's place. There were still a few police cars there. Seeing them struck me as interesting. This guy with the shotgun never once asked what was going on at the duplex. Wouldn't he want to know?

Or was this a sign that he already did?

5

*A*fter everything that had happened with poor Charlie, it was discouraging to admit I was nearly in the same depressed mental space that Carlson had originally found me. The spiral downward had started soon after I'd returned home. I'd been super bummed I'd lost my notebook. Why had I forgotten it at the duplex? Obviously, my head still wasn't in the game. I'd gone to bed filled with a resolve that I would get it back.

All of that fell apart by morning, when I couldn't summon the will-power to get out of bed. Desolation sang its hypnotic song to me... "Just hide away. There's nothing you can do to fix things." I rubbed my feet against the sheets and covered my head with the quilt to hide from the sun.

It didn't do any good. Having to pee eventually forced me from my warm cocoon.

I stumbled into the bathroom, took care of business, and then had a drink from the faucet. It was the reflection staring back from the mirror as I wiped my mouth that finally snapped me out of it.

It was scary. Not that my face, with sheet-print wrinkles and puffy hair was scary, but how quickly those dark emotions had returned to drag me back under.

I shook my head. No. I wasn't going back to that place. I was strong, and I was going to get my moxie back. I flipped on the shower, forcing myself in before the water had warmed entirely.

The shock of cold helped. I scrubbed my hair and face. I even shaved my legs and used my extra special lotion when I got out.

After I got dressed, I grabbed my sneakers from behind the door. *Okay, girl. Let's go fight.*

———

It was a long road. I couldn't see the end, what with the dust blowing. I'd only been out here twenty minutes and already my clothing, skin, and mouth were caked with it. In a way, I didn't care about the dust that coated me. The entire inside of my soul had felt gritty and gross for a while, so I guess my outsides finally matched.

My feet pounded the ground. With each step I said my mother's name. I'd sure been in some crazy situations in my life. Circumstances where I even impressed myself at this weird bravery I'd discovered deep in my core. However, when it came to my mom, I'd been running from the truth, afraid to face any real emotions the thought of her evoked.

When my uncle finally told me that my mom was in prison, the betrayal I'd felt caused me to hide again, this time behind anger.

Anger was a good mask. The only problem was that it soon slid into despondency and loss of hope because I still hadn't dealt with what the anger was masking.

I wasn't going to hide under bed quilts anymore. I was out here to make my muscles scream and lungs burn, to run the anger off in a clean sweat and clear thoughts.

It would have worked, too, if a tractor hadn't pulled out at the end of the road, leaving me to follow it back home. I swear, there was almost as much dirt stirred up in the air as there was on the road.

Although the tractor drove out of sight, I could still hear its engines growl from some place far ahead. My feet ate up the ground, my muscles reminding me that I was strong. I could handle all of this drama.

Strong. Strong. Strong.

I slowed to a cool down, lacing my fingers behind my neck, and breathed in. My sweat left a sheen on my arms, bare despite the brisk temperature on this sunny morning.

My Uncle Chris. My dad. Even my grandfather, Oscar. I couldn't hide from them forever. It broke my heart to think of how hopeful I'd been about reuniting Oscar with his two sons. How I'd relished feeling like I finally had a family, after it being just dad and me for so long. Yet, all this time, I'd been trying to protect my family against the enemies of the world, not realizing I was actually in camp with them.

"Stella?" a man called.

I jerked to a stop and turned. It was Richie, my neighbor who owned the farm down the street. I realized then that I had just passed his house. He was walking through the field with a pick, showing off some mighty fine forearm muscles, his face shielded from the sun by a cowboy hat. I couldn't help but notice how tight his sleeves were through the biceps as well.

Stella, you're staring. "Uh, hi," I answered, trying to sound cute. A tickle ran down my cheek and I brushed it away, hoping it was sweat and not a bug. My hands flew to my hair where I realized my ponytail had turned into a hot mess. I was cute all right, about as cute as a pile of snarled dental floss.

His eyes studied me, his own dark hair brushing the back of his shirt's neckline. "How are you? I haven't seen you in a while. And then I saw the cop stop by yesterday." He cleared his throat as if embarrassed even though his gaze remained intense. "I was worried."

I was surprised he'd noticed my absence, and honestly, a bit flattered. There was no time to savor his words. I was being asked some questions that needed thoughtful answers.

"Oh, that," I hemmed, trying to figure out how to start. How does one explain a situation like this without sounding crazy? "I guess I've been holed up in my house for a while. Kind of got dealt a blow, and I've been trying to cope with it."

Lines formed between his eyebrows as he leaned against the pick. "What? Are you okay?"

Oh no! He's worried! Hurriedly, I continued. "No, I'm fine. Just... family dysfunction at its best. Some days, you never know what to expect."

He nodded, his face relaxing. "Every family has it to some degree. Even me and my mom." He shrugged.

"Things changed after Dad died. You have to figure it out, keep the peace as best as you can. Life is short, really. It is."

"Yeah, well..." I shrugged. He didn't understand what I was going through. Still, a tiny voice nudged me that my own dad wasn't getting any younger. The bigger part of me, the part that didn't want to forgive raged at the tiny voice until I squashed it into submission.

"You want to talk about it?" he asked, his hand easing down the pick handle.

It was such an intense story, my mom, dad and Uncle Chris. He would never believe me. Besides, did I really want to put those thoughts in his head about me? That my mom was some sort of convict and my grandfather was the one that arrested her? That my dad moved us to Seattle to shake the dust from his feet?

I nodded. "Yeah."

"Well, come on in. I know mom will be excited to see you."

We had a little mix up where I didn't know if I should follow him through the field, or if he was coming out onto the street to walk back up the road. It ended with a few giggles, and he stepped onto the road.

"I wouldn't want you to have to trek through that in your nice shoes," he said, slinging the pick onto his shoulder. Broad shoulders. Very, very broad shoulders.

The gravel crunched under our feet, highlighting a few awkward seconds of being unsure of how to start a conversation between us.

Finally, he began. "It's so beautiful out here. You know, working in the city, I didn't realize how much I missed this."

"How's your business going?" I asked, knowing he owned an automobile shop and had recently reopened it in his barn.

"Good. My old customers seem to want to stay loyal. That really helps."

"You usually work on cars with that?" I pointed to the pick with a smile.

He laughed. "Getting the fields ready for planting. There were a few huge rocks that popped up out of nowhere."

I nodded, and the silence descended once again. This time I broke it. "Hey, I wanted to thank you, for dinner the other night." He'd seen me at the Springfield Diner a few weeks ago and had dropped some money off with the waitress, telling her to pay for my meal. It had caused some confusion for a while about some anonymous man spying on me until Marla Springfield cleared it up.

"What? Aww, no problem. You looked like you were having a

hard day." He removed his cowboy hat with a suave flex of his arm and brushed his hair from his forehead, before replacing the hat with a practiced jerk.

I usually didn't like long hair on men, however it looked good on him. Real good. He stared at me with dark, almond-shaped eyes and smiled.

Okay, I'm staring again. This is embarrassing. To give myself time to regroup, I bent down to tie my shoe. "It was so nice of you. I didn't find out who did it until last week, though. The waitress didn't share your name." I didn't bother to tell him the waitress hated me and had made him appear as creepy as possible.

"She wasn't supposed to. I just appreciated the kindness you've given to my mom and wanted to pass it along."

"What? Your mom's so nice. It's no problem at all."

He smiled. "She gets a little confused sometimes, especially since dad died, but she's the sweetest, most generous, kindest person in the world."

I smiled. He had no idea how cute he was being right now. I decided to try on my flirting game. "I heard you bought my car."

"Your car?"

By now we reached his driveway and were heading down to

the white farmhouse.

"Yeah, the purple Challenger I'd been eyeing for a while," I answered. The front door opened then, and I swear I could smell vanilla.

"Richie!" Mrs. Wilson came out. She had on a pink apron and a big smile. "You brought Stella back."

"Hi, Mrs. Wilson," I said.

"Oh, we're past that now. Please call me Truly."

"Truly?"

She laughed softy, the sound reminding me of the wind brushing flower petals in a garden. She was in much better spirits since the last time I'd seen her. "Yep. Now come in!"

I did go in, and we visited for a while. Richie and I never got back to our conversation, though I could tell he wanted to. Truly was enjoying my company so much, I didn't dare leave. First, she took me down memory lane with a photo album. Richie rolled his eyes and shifted uncomfortably from where he leaned against the door frame like it was his duty to keep it propped up. He was an adorable kid, and it was my first time seeing his sister, who Truly missed very much. After a few cookies and a tour through the living room to see her latest dolls, I finally made my goodbyes.

It made me sad to see how lonely Truly was. I felt for Richie as well. The hole her husband had left behind was huge, and as hard as Richie tried, I knew he wouldn't be able to fill it.

My mental wheels turned as I headed back to my house. I should have been jogging again, but with a full belly and a more peaceful mind, I wasn't in the mood.

As I walked, my eye caught sight of my sneaker tread, with its corkscrew print. It made me wonder about the one at Charlie Booker's house. It struck me now that I'd noticed it on my return trip when I had the contract for Charlie to sign, not when I'd taken Gary Davis for the showing.

Then there was the disturbing news the dog neighbor had shared about people traveling through the woods behind his house. Maybe they were clues. Someone should know about it.

I fished my phone from my pant's pocket and hit the button for Officer Carlson. He *had* said I could call any time.

"Hollywood," he answered after the fifth ring. "You doing okay?"

I smiled. "Hi, Carlson. I'm doing better." I hesitated and then blurted. "Thank you for coming yesterday. It shook me out of my pity-trip."

"Hey, we all need a shake or two every now and then. What's going on?"

"Well, speaking of shake ups. Did you hear about Charlie Booker? He was murdered yesterday. And I was there."

"Fancy you being there," he said, dryly, reminding me that even though he might show compassion, he was no push-over. And, apparently, he believed I had a penchant for stumbling into trouble.

"His house was for sale. I'd shown the place earlier and had an offer for him to sign. Anyway, I saw some shoe prints during my second trip. I'm not sure if anyone else noticed them or not."

"What sort of shoe prints?" he asked.

"Athletic shoes. I have a pair myself so I recognized the tread. They appeared to be men's, judging by the size."

"All right, I'll look into it and get back to you if we have any more questions. In the meantime, you take care of yourself, you hear?"

"I will. I am."

"Unless you want me to do another welfare check on you," he added, his voice deeper.

Was he...? He *was* flirting with me! I smiled, thinking how I'd finally won him over. "I'm doing much better, now. Don't worry."

He snorted. "Worry's my middle name apparently, when it comes to you." His voice hinted heavily and I wondered if he was referring to our past experience at the Heritage Dispensary. As I hung up, the memory of the time he'd shot his pistol over my shoulder rang in my head.

---

6

*B*y the time I made it home, I'd decided what my next step would be. I was going to get my journal back. It was ridiculous to think it was gone forever. Charlie's sister was staying with him. Maybe I could just swing by and see if she was home.

But first, there was another idea I had brewing in the back of my mind. As I drove to Charlie Booker's duplex, I click "Talk," on my steering wheel and asked for Charity Valentine.

Charity was a woman somewhere in her late seventies/early eighties. I'd helped to sell her family manor when I first moved here.

The phone rang through the car's speakers. It was picked up with a peppy, "Hello!"

"Hi, Charity. It's Stella."

"Stella! How are you?" Her voice oozed with bubbly enthusiasm.

"I'm good. I had a favor to ask you. I hope you don't mind. Are you still volunteering at the nursing home?"

"Yes! I am! Tuesday night is Bingo. Plus, there's my honey...." She giggled as she left the thought dangling.

"Aww, you're still with him. That's great. Listen, I have a friend whose mom is kind of lonely ever since her husband died. Do you think you could invite her to Bingo one night?"

"Of course!" Charity said brightly. "There's always room for one more! Plus we have prizes. Last week was a shaker mug with a protein pack."

A protein pack? I shook it off. *Never mind.* "Her name is Truly Wilson, and she might have a few memory issues. However, she's such a sweet lady, and I think you'll really like her."

"Well, at our age, who doesn't have memory issues?"

Warmth filled my chest at her friendliness. I rattled of the

Wilson phone number, hoping I wasn't crossing a boundary, and she promised to call soon. Apparently, tomorrow was pancake breakfast, so Charity couldn't wait to see if Truly was interested.

Feeling very good about how that phone call went, I hung up and then concentrated on changing gears. Operation notebook was set to go.

It was weird being back at the duplex after seeing it cordoned off yesterday with yellow tape. The driveway was empty of cars which caused my heart to sink. Still, I hoped that maybe Maribel's car was in the garage. Puffing my cheeks with a deep breath, I climbed out of the car and walked to the front door. I knocked hard, feeling slightly bad about disturbing Charlie's sister at such a sad time.

There was a twitch of the neighbor's curtains, something I was becoming accustomed to. I waved at the peering face near the top third of the window, and then pounded on the door again.

This time it opened, and the woman with the dark curly hair stared at me blankly. It was odd. No 'Can I help you?' or 'Hello.'

She's grieving, I reminded myself. "Hi, there. My name is Stella O'Neil. I am—was—the real estate agent trying to sell your brother's place."

She gave no response that she'd heard me. Not even a blink of the eyes. Honestly, her wooden stare was starting to spook me a little. I cleared my throat. "Um, I'm so sorry to hear about Charlie."

Her nostrils twitched at the mention of her brother's name.

"I don't want to keep you. I left a book here. I feel horrible about bothering you, but I need it back."

"Book?"

"It had a purple cover. You were carrying it yesterday."

She looked down at her hand as if remembering. "Yeah, I left it in my car. My boyfriend has it. He just ran to the store."

The seconds trickled by, with her standing like a mannequin, and me blinking like a llama that's just been denied some hay.

I tried to switch gears through the disappointment. "Should I come back later, then? Maybe sometime around six?"

"Look, I don't want to talk about it anymore. You work at the realty, right? The one with the Flamingo? I'll drop it off when he gets back."

I clenched my jaw, hating how out-of-control this situation had become. I just needed my notebook. Who knew if she'd follow through? It didn't matter now since there was nothing more I could do. With a quick nod and a thank you, I stepped off the porch and back to the walkway. "Well, I'll see you then. And remember, it's no trouble for me to swing by to get it."

"We'll talk later. I've got something in the oven," she said firmly.

I lifted my hand to say goodbye, but she was already shutting the door.

Something in the oven? Her brother just died—was murdered —and she was baking something? But what did I know? People grieved in mysterious ways. I remembered how Kari had said Maribel hadn't wanted to move and had sabotaged the showing. Maybe, in a small way, she was comforted she was staying.

Back in my car, I rubbed my neck to release some anxiety, before glancing at the duplex. Was that neighbor watching me right now?

The duplex units were connected by a shared wall between the two offices. As I stared at the connection point, that little mental itch started again... something about it bothered me.

The building appeared normal, in a very elementary modern style. At the connection point were two windows, one for each duplex, separated by a large expanse of brick facing.

Something was off. But what?

My baby hairs tickled at the base of my neck. I glanced down to the living room on the other side of the duplex. Sure enough, the louvers in one of the windows snapped shut. The neighbor had been at it again.

Spying.

Weird. I started the car and drove the thirty minutes back to the Flamingo Realty. To pass the time, I tried to come up with a list of suspects who might have killed Charlie Booker. He had that strange security system that seemed like overkill at the time. I mentally winced at my use of the word 'kill'. Obviously, he had been paranoid, and it seemed for a good reason. Maribel, his sister was acting so strangely. After a solid week of binge watching American Detective, there was no denying that in most cases, the closest loved one was the guilty party. There was her boyfriend too, some mysterious man who was driving around with my notebook in his car. When did he come into the picture? Did he live there now?

Frustration made me growl as I parked in front of the realty. I stormed in and slammed the door. The little bell tinkled cheerfully in the most annoying way.

Kari glanced up from her desk. Her short, blonde hair was pulled back somewhat haphazardly in a twist, and her face was pale.

"Good morning," she whispered.

I stopped dead in my tracks. "Kari, are you okay?"

She nodded and then half-heartedly lifted a shoulder. "Stay back. The kids got me sick, those little Petri dishes. I'm just here to file this last bit of paperwork and then I'm headed home." A frown fluttered across her face. "And what about you? You walked in here like there's a storm brewing."

I sighed and tossed my purse on my desk. "I just got back from the duplex."

She frowned. "I heard. I can't believe that happened! The poor guy."

"Well, in an odd twist of things, that duplex still isn't out of my life. I left one of my notebooks there. Yesterday, the sister had it in her hand when she was talking with the police. She practically hit the officer in the chest with it."

"What? Are you serious?"

"Yeah, she was super agitated. I thought for sure she was going to get arrested and I was never going to see it again. Then she disappeared, so I thought I'd stop by today and try to pick it up. She gave me a song and dance about how she left it in the car that her boyfriend took. The whole thing was weird."

Kari fanned her face with a flyer. "What was weird?"

"I can't put my finger on it. Her reaction seemed very off. And then there was something else. Gary actually brought it up when I was showing the house. One of the rooms seemed extra small. I thought it was because of all the boxes stacked against the wall."

"Boxes? Kari arched an eyebrow at me. "Sounds like maybe Charlie was thinking of moving. Or was it Maribel trying to do a little sabotage again?"

"I don't think it was her. The rest of the place was clean. Here, let me show you." I grabbed a pen and a junk mail envelope. I flipped it over for a blank spot to sketch. "Look." With a few simple lines, I drew the duplex, drawing and redrawing the lines where they connected. "See here where the window is? There should be a space on the other side, making the window in the center of the wall. Yet, when you're inside, the window is right next to the corner."

"Huh. Well, maybe they redesigned it?" The flyer was practically a blur as her fanning took on a tinge of desperation.

I studied my drawing. "I guess so. Maybe they turned it into an extra closet." I hadn't seen one, but that didn't mean it wasn't there. I could have been distracted. "I don't know. Anyway, you can head out if you want. I'll man the office, especially since I don't have any more clients. Again," I added dryly.

"They'll come. Don't worry, you'll build up a list. Thanks,

because I really do need to get out of here. My stomach is threatening to reveal what I had for breakfast, I can tell. And maybe throw in my shoes for good measure."

I wrinkled my nose as Kari gathered her things. "Call if you need me."

After she left, I went online and scrolled through Brookfield's community page to see if anyone had lost their dog. There was one request, for a black lab named Rex. My fingers flew across the keys as I typed a post describing how I'd found a collar for a dog named Nymph if anyone was missing it, and then hit send.

After that, curiosity forced me to go to the city's website and check for the housing plans submitted for the duplex. The address was new so the permits came up easily.

I clicked the link and expanded the picture, focusing on the connecting rooms between the duplexes. There was no closet against that wall. In fact, the room was dubbed an office on the plans, just like it was in the listing.

He had to have made that space into a closet then, and he must have done it without permits. That was nothing new. People did things like that all the time.

So why did it bother me so much?

I leaned back in the chair, causing it to squeak, which in turn made me glance toward Uncle Chris's office. His door was shut. Did he know I was out here... what was he thinking?

I wanted to be petty and say I didn't care what he thought. Instead, my mind drifted toward the night when he'd finally confessed about my mom. I'd run out of the restaurant, too overwhelmed to process anything else. I realized now that I wanted to know more.

Had Uncle Chris been in love with my mother as well? Had he known she was going to that party? Why hadn't he stopped her or told my dad? Even worse, did Dad know my mom had returned to drugs, and if so, why hadn't he tried to help her?

"You can't get a lot of answers when you're not talking to people," I whispered.

Uncle Chris cleared his throat loudly from behind his closed door, answering my earlier question. My back stiffened. This was it... the moment I could get some questions answered.

My phone rang, bringing a wave of relief. I grabbed it like a safety rope being thrown over a cliff.

"Hello?" I answered.

It was Carlson. "Hey, I have some info about the shoe tracks. Unfortunately, it seems any signs of prints were obscured by the foot traffic that came from the ambulance. We do have a partial at the edge of the sidewalk, however, it's not enough to be identifying."

"Maybe I could find a picture on line and show you what it looks like."

"What are you? The great shoe detective?" he responded a little hotly.

That popped my eyes open. "What's the matter with you?" I asked.

He groaned. "I'm sorry. It was a long night, and I'm exhausted."

"What's going on?" It was none of my business, but the question slipped out.

"Well, have you heard about the chain of delivery truck robberies recently? That's the case I'm working on."

I paused for a second. "You don't suppose...."

"Suppose what?"

"That's what happened to Charlie? A robbery gone wrong?"

"Last I looked, his house wasn't a delivery truck."

I rolled my eyes at his acerbic tone but bit my tongue. He did say he was tired. Besides, I was distracted by Uncle Chris walking through the office with a pile of mail.

Hurriedly, I adverted my face so we wouldn't make eye contact. He left for the mailbox with the front door jingling.

Carlson continued. "Besides, his sister said that even though the house was ransacked and the huge TV yanked off the wall, only the laptop was missing."

"Who would go through the trouble of destroying a TV instead of stealing it?" I asked.

"Yeah, it's odd, but then again, thieves aren't known for being too bright. Anyway, the good news is that it looks like we've got this case close to being buttoned up."

"Really? That was fast."

"Makes me relieved. You know what they say about the first twenty-four hours."

"What do they say?"

"It's when most murder suspects are identified. Anyway, that's all I'm at liberty to discuss. We'll get this sorted out."

"Well, there's one more thing. I ended up talking with one of the neighbor's who mentioned that there'd been a lot of people running through the woods behind his house."

"Interesting. Which neighbor was that?"

I gave him directions as best as I could, which boiled down to me describing it as a weird driveway through a tunnel of bushes.

"Got it. If you think of anything else, let me know." He paused and then added, "Maybe we can talk in person?"

Did I detect a wistful note in that burly cop's voice? "Sounds good. I'll bring doughnuts," I teased.

"Good. I like the kind with chocolate sprinkles."

He hung up as I laughed.

7

I continued to smile, although I'll admit, the thought of doughnuts made my stomach growl. I scrolled through my work emails, including sending an email to Gary Davis to update him with a few more town homes that might work for him instead. I'm sure he was disappointed, but there was nothing more I could do with the Charlie Booker place.

The front door opened with the tinkle of the bell. Uncle Chris returned, his steps heavy. My eyebrows rose, and I quickly glanced away. He looked like he'd aged ten years since the night at the restaurant.

I wanted to stay mad, but seeing him so sad was messing with my anger, darn it. I stared hard at my screen like I was decoding a bomb threat, trying to ignore my softening resolve.

He walked closer. Sweat sprang out along my scalp line. *Please go away. Not today, Uncle Chris. I decided I'm not ready.*

"Stella," His voice creaked like it hadn't been much in use. "There's something that came for you."

I glanced up. *Finally! My notebook!* I guess Charlie's sister had dropped it off, after all. My excitement must have shown on my face because Uncle Chris raised a corner of his lip in a hopeful smile.

"It was a letter," he clarified, handing over a stiff white envelope. Uneasily, he shifted his weight to one foot as he squeezed his hands. The sound like small sticks breaking came as he cracked his knuckles. "Is there anything I can help with?" he asked.

I shook my head as a surge of disappointment swelled into anger that wanted to be unleashed. It sorely wanted to make a target out of him. I pressed my lips together to be sure I didn't say anything that I might regret later.

"Okay, then. Just let me know. I'm here to talk." After a second, he walked away. His office door shut softly.

I tore into the envelope. Inside was a sheet of paper with colorful magazine letters glued to it. What in the world was this? It looked just like an elementary student's homework who had been given the assignment, "Make a ransom note."

I was so distracted by the absurdity that I half-smiled as I read it. The smile quickly dropped away.

DEAR STELLA

Everyone sees how you

are snooping. Keep your nose clean and focus on your own

details.

Death comes

roaring with a vengeance

if you don't mind your own business,

finding family far and wide,

touching everyone loved by a snoop.

"KARI!" I shouted. No answer. I glanced around the office. Shoot! I'd forgotten she wasn't there.

A tentative cough came from the back of the office. "Is there anything I can help you with, Stella?"

This was it. After this moment, I'd no longer be able to ignore him any longer. Groaning in protest, I shoved the chair back and walked into my uncle's office.

"I need you to look at this." I held out the letter. "Where did you find it at?"

"It was under your windshield wiper."

This was the most we'd communicated since that dreadful meeting at the restaurant. I was oddly comforted by being around him.

His face flushed as he scanned the paper. "Oh, boy. Not liking this at all. We need to call the cops."

"Yeah, I plan to do that next," I said, reaching for it back.

"I'll check the records. There's got to be something on them."

"The records?"

"Yeah, the cameras are on a twenty-four-hour loop. We'll catch whoever did this."

"Is this something I can watch as well? I mean, maybe I'll recognize the person."

"Great idea. I'll send you the password so you can log in. Actually, you should have it anyway, being that this is your family's business."

I heard that reminder in his voice, maybe it was a plea. I couldn't leave it hanging. I didn't want to face the emotions, but this wasn't getting us anywhere.

"Listen, it's been a lot to process, the talk we had," I began.

His face softened. "You have every right to be angry."

"Well, I think I'm mostly confused. I do have questions. I'm not ready to talk about it now."

"Grill away, Stella. I'll answer anything. I love you. We all do."

"Thank you. We'll talk soon, just as soon as I deal with this mess." I tapped the envelope against the desk.

"You be careful! Maybe we should hire security."

"It could be some dumb prank," I said as I started to walk out of his office. "I mean, it's not even a real threat."

Still, back at my desk, the first thing I did was text Officer Carlson.

—**I got this dropped off today.** I took a careful picture of the letter and sent it to him.

He seemed to take it seriously, or maybe he was on a break and bored monitoring motorists because he responded right away. —**Let's meet at the Springfield Diner. You game?**

—**When?** I asked.

—**How about for lunch?**

—Sounds good.

There. I'd bring the letter to him then. I pulled my keyboard over. In the meantime, I could study the security videos. I checked my messages for the password.

"Uncle Chris! Can you send the password!" I reminded him.

"You bet!" he answered, that relief still active in his voice.

He was happy I was talking to him again. I don't know how I felt. Still angry. Resigned to the fact that I needed to figure it out because I needed this job. Maybe I was a little relieved as well. I mean, life had to go on.

A moment later, I logged into the site and started scrolling through the latest videos of action. What, I'd been here over an hour already? I could see myself walk in to the realty. I cringed at the expression on my face. It was defensive and scared.

I hit rewind. I could just see the corner of my car. Why had I decided to park there? Oh wait... what was that? A pair of legs, the upper body cut off from the camera, approached my car. Had they followed me? They were about to come into view. My breath caught in my chest. Here they come...just a little closer.

A sparkle and a blur of a hand flashed over my windshield, leaving a white envelope like a leaf. No face.

Disappointed, I pushed back from the computer. The film was too blurry to make out if it was a man or a woman. Then I took out my phone and paused the film to take a picture. Maybe I could mess with it in editing.

I glanced at the time. Seeing it was close to noon, I grabbed the envelope with the letter and headed out to meet Officer Carlson.

8

I found a spot to park right in the front of the Springfield Diner. I smiled like I'd just won the lottery. The jaunty red-and-white striped awnings snapped in the cool breeze. The staff had been busy since the last time I'd been by and all of the red flower boxes had been freshly painted and filled with colorful Gerber Daisies. A hummingbird buzzed from one to another.

There was a flutter in my stomach, much like the jeweled-head hummingbird before me. What was this? Was I... nervous?

Oh man, what was going on? Was I actually feeling butterflies over seeing the burly cop? A man with hands like ham slices, a bald head, and a scowl that could make a mime confess? A man who always teased me?

I spied the white envelope peeking out of my purse. This was ridiculous. What was I thinking? He was only here to get the threatening letter.

Still, I wasn't taking any chances after the last time he'd seen me looking like a cheese chip monster. I pulled the visor down and checked myself in the mirror. *Pinch the cheeks and get some lipstick.* I fumbled for my tinted chapstick and quickly applied it before smoothing my hair back. I pressed my lips together and nodded in approval. Okay. Let's get this show on the road.

Letter in hand, I headed for the diner. Mrs. Springfield, the owner, was just inside the door as I walked in, a spry woman who ran this place with an iron rule since the restaurant's doors first opened over fifty years earlier. Well into her eighties, she had a bounce in her step that was quite remarkable, considering her white thick-soled shoes looked like concrete blocks on the ends of her skinny legs.

"Well, now. Stella! You here for my rhubarb pie? I have some rhubarb I froze last year that was fresh from my garden."

Good heavens, she gardened too? That woman was as busy as that hummingbird outside.

I shook my head. "No, I'm here to meet someone for lunch."

"Oh!" Her wizened face took on a knowing expression, and

her eyes sparkled in humor. "I should have guessed. Your young man, right? He's here."

My young man? Was she saying Carlson...?

"Let me take you back," she said, all business. She whisked a menu from the desk and started to walk, her shoes soundless against the flooring.

I followed after her, completely caught off guard. Was it that obvious how Carlson felt? He must have a thing for me! He did seem a little flirty that one time I saw him. Had he said something to her?

She led me to a table, and my feet tripped over one another.

It was Richie, my neighbor.

He glanced up from his menu and seemed as surprised as I was. He hid it well behind a big grin. "Stella! What are you doing here?"

That definitely caught Mrs. Springfield off guard. "Oh, I thought she was here to meet you." And then her hand landed on my arm, as light as a frail butterfly. "I am so sorry."

"It's okay, I'm actually here to meet Officer Carslon. What are you doing, grabbing lunch?" Okay, not my best comeback, but at least I'd recovered enough to fake it. Mentally I was berating myself for letting my imagination take me away *again* about Carlson.

Richie's dark eyes flicked around the tables as if looking for the cop. I did too, and spotted him by the window. Carlson had been watching me and acknowledged my gaze by lifting a hand and giving a wry smile.

"Ahh," Richie's smile flickered. "Are you here to...?"

"Oh, some official police business," I said. I lifted the envelope as if that would be explanation enough.

"Great." Relief came back in the form of that confident light in his eyes. "I just got done dropping Mom off for a ladies lunch."

"Really?"

"Yeah." His head tilted and a gentle smile curved his lips. "This is good timing to see you since I've been wanting to thank you. Maybe when you're done with your official police business, we could have lunch?" He brushed his hair off his forehead in an exaggerated stretch.

Now I was all confused. All I could get out was, "Thank me?" Embarrassingly, it came out as a squeak.

"Yeah. For what you're doing for Ma. You sent the Valentine sisters, didn't you?"

Sisters? "I called Charity Valentine. She's a friend of mine. I wanted to see if she had time to visit."

"Well, they came and had a good chat with mom. After lunch, they're whisking her away to play Bingo. I haven't seen Ma so happy in a long time."

My heart warmed. "I'm so glad. Charity is a sweetheart." I didn't add anything about Gladys Valentine, her older, sterner sister. My run-ins with Gladys hadn't been nearly so pleasant. In fact, I was quite surprised to hear she had joined Charity for lunch.

From across the restaurant, Carlson called, "Stella! Times' ticking! I've got to get back!"

My cheeks heated.

"I'll leave you two be," said Marla.

I jerked, surprised she was still there. Oh, she sure was, innocent eyes blinking while she tallied this whole embarrassing affair into her gossip bank. I'm sure the tale would be twisted somehow to become some torrid love story of me caught between two men. I cringed at the thought and gave an awkward goodbye to Richie, telling him to enjoy his lunch, before hurrying over to Carlson.

"Hi, I'm so sorry," I said as I slid into the seat across from the cop. He watched me with an amused smile.

"Are you one of those people you can't take anywhere

without getting into a million conversations because you know everyone?"

"What? No. That's my neighbor. He was just giving me an update about his mom."

Carlson rolled his shoulders. "Well, I have some good news of my own. We picked up that gang I was telling you about. And guess what. One of them had on athletic shoes like you described."

"What? Really! That's incredible!"

The waitress brought over some water and took our order. I was surprised when Carlson ordered his burger medium rare. But why should I be? The man looked like he wrangled cows with his bare hands.

After she left, I continued. "So the murder investigation is over, just like that."

"Not, 'just like that', Hollywood. We have this thing called due process. Right at this moment, I'm sure the prosecutors are trying to secure a confession with some sort of plea deal."

"How's it going?"

He shrugged casually, but his brow rumpled in a curious way. "These things take time."

"Why do you look a little unsure?"

He squinted his eyes, "I'm a little worried because they had a pipe bomb in the trunk of their car when they were captured. It was a scary moment for the arresting officers. I'm hoping there aren't any more bombs hidden out there. I'm just glad we got them off the streets."

Well, that was eerie. "Any more?"

"The bombs... we'll see what the interrogation uncovers. Now, what is it you got today?"

I jumped at the reminder of why we were meeting and slid over the letter.

He winced and took the envelope with his napkin.

"Oh, fingerprints...." I said.

"Good thing we have yours on file," he remarked with a flicker of his eyebrow. He opened it and read. His nostrils widened. "You have any idea who could have left this?"

I shook my head.

"See anyone around?"

"No. I did look at the surveillance tape from the realty. Hard to see anything on it though."

He nodded and tucked the letter in his leather folder. "I'll stop by and have a look. It could be nothing. In fact, it's so amateurish, it looks like a prank. Some competitor trying to scare you. Still, keep an eye out. Let me know if you see anything out of the ordinary."

I nodded. "You got it."

The waitress brought our food, and I tucked into it like I was competing for the fastest French fry eating contest before decorum reminded me to chill out. Carlson didn't seem to notice. The rest of our meal was spent talking about how he got into the police force. Apparently, he had been in the military first, along with his good buddy, Frank Wagner. Frank was a police officer himself now, and suggested Carlson become one as well.

This explained so much of Carlson's crusty demeanor. He was tough. He had seen things. He was dependable. It was nice to see him soften as he talked about his fellow soldier and friend.

I mostly listened. He poked a little bit at my reasons why I'd moved to Brookfield. I hedged, my mother still fresh in my mind. All the reasons I used to give—that I'd come to reestablish a relationship with the rest of my family—couldn't be shared with any great conviction. I ended up giving some lame explanation that I really liked the area.

It *was* a beautiful place, but even he didn't believe that I'd leave my life behind in Seattle to come out here to start over with nothing. His eyebrows raised but he didn't press anymore.

At some point, Richie left, giving me a gentle wave across the room. I swear, I saw Carlson smirk, the expression dropping quickly when he saw me looking.

"Do you know him?" I asked curiously.

He shook his head. "No, other than the rumor that he's extremely good at what he does. Rebuilding engines and such. A couple of my buddies might have clocked him out on the back roads driving his hot rod like a banshee was on his tail. He knows his way around and has never been caught."

I thought of how Richie just bought that purple Challenger that I had wanted. I knew if I had succeeded in getting my hands on it, I'd be taking it for speed tests as well.

Carlson wiped his mouth and took a sip of water. He gave me an easy grin. "Thanks for meeting me. I had fun."

My hand froze with a French fry in mid-air. Wait. Was this a date? I glanced over to see what might be the same nervousness I felt being reflected in his big smile.

Oh, my gosh. He likes me. I knew it! I quickly pumped the brakes before I gave my feelings away, forcing my facial expression to demonstrate being cool as a cucumber.

"It was fun," I calmly answered. I was pretty proud of my

response considering how he'd taken me off guard.

He fished out his wallet, and I scrambled for mine.

"Don't even think about it," he said.

"I'm thinking about it," I answered, sliding out my card.

"I invited you. My treat." He held a couple of bills in the air with two fingers, glancing for the waitress.

She came over and took them, leaving my card ignored on the table.

"Well, thank you," I said.

He stood, causing his leather boots to creak. "You take care of yourself, Hollywood. I'll look into the security tapes and figure out who left the letter." He tapped his leather folder.

He walked me to the door where we awkwardly separated with our cars parked in opposite directions.

I waved as he drove past, feeling pretty good. Charlie Booker's murderer had been caught, and things were on a better track with me and Uncle Chris. Sure, there were still issues with Dad and Oscar, but life was settling down once again.

I flipped on the radio, and "Foolish Lies" blasted through the speakers. I sang along as I pulled out onto the road. Little did I know I was singing my own ironic theme song.

9

There was nothing left for me to do at the office so I went home, and ended up spending the rest of the evening laying more of the flooring. It was time to get the job done, and I was pleased that I had most of it finished by bedtime, except for the last bit which needed some complicated cuts.

The next morning, armed with a mug of coffee, I stared out the kitchen window at a few fat robins bouncing about the yard, and relished finally feeling like myself again. While watching the birds, a clear memory came of me at about eight-years-old. I'd thought I was being clever by asking my dad, "Is it true that the early bird always catches the worm?"

"That's right," he'd said, apparently pleased that the virtue was firmly planted in my brain. "It's why you want to get up early, ready to tackle the day and—"

"But, Dad," I'd interrupted. "What about the worm? After all, wasn't he up early, too?"

He'd paused for a moment, and I'd giggled at finally having stumped him. Then he'd answered emphatically, "It was really a late night worm."

I smiled at the memory. Dad had thought he was being so tricky. Steam wafted around me as I brought the mug up for another sip.

Then, something magical happened. Through the mist at the edge of the property, where the wild forest joined the soggy grass, a tentative head poked into sight.

A deer. I squealed softly in delight. Thin, jerky movements followed the deer. The mist parted to reveal her speckled fawn.

"Oh, my gosh, she's bringing him here!" I jumped up and walked to the back door, quietly easing it opened.

Momma deer wasn't fooled. She stared straight at me.

I huddled behind the door frame, trying to blend in. The fawn froze behind its mom. Dark, liquid brown eyes watched me curiously as its ears flicked forward.

"Hi, handsome," I whispered.

The deer studied me a few more seconds before moving forward on slender legs. Momma deer's dark nose dipped into the clover and baby did the same.

I could barely hold back a giggle. Some mornings it was easy to recognize the privilege of being alive. This was definitely one of them.

I watched the pair until the cold morning air made me shiver. Spring was here, but it still wasn't warm, at least at this time of day. The noise of me reentering the house and shutting the door was enough to encourage the duo to slip back into the trees. I wondered if I'd see them again.

I refilled the mug and took it to the couch, squashy with overstuffed cushions. After burrowing into the sofa—coffee mug sitting on the window sill—I opened the browser on the laptop. I wanted to watch the realty's security footage again. Maybe there was something I missed.

Instead, what confronted me was a news article.

Gang captured as suspects to the murder of a local man. Bomb found.

Below it were the mug shots of the four thieves, a height marker behind them measuring them under six feet. They all appeared young—in their early twenties—each one giving the camera surly glares. I studied the photos but didn't recognize any of the men from the group of spectators hanging around the house that day. I was a firm believer that the murderer always came back to the crime scene. Still, one of them could have been skirting the edges of the property, and I would have never noticed.

Cold-blooded murderers. I shook my head and logged into the Flamingo Realty security site to view the footage one more time. Slowly, I wound the piece, frame by frame, chewing the edge of my thumbnail. How was it that we could see details on the moon, yet technology hadn't made a security camera sharp enough to give more than a grainy image?

I studied the footage again. Ninety percent of the scene was of the person's legs. This time something caught my attention. Huge athletic running shoes.

A prickle ran down my spine. They were the same brand of sneakers that I owned. The same brand as the print I'd seen leading into Charlie Booker's house the other day.

They must be the guy that Carlson had in custody. But something about the shot was bothering me.

I ran the film again. This time I zoomed in on something else. The envelope being stuck behind the windshield wiper; a flash on the hand. There was something else there... a pink smear in the glass. I knew exactly what it was.

The reflection of the person's face.

But no amount of zooming would make it any clearer. I closed the laptop and took a sip of my now-cold coffee. Grimacing, I dumped it in the sink and got ready to head out.

I had one more plan before I started my day.

FORTY MINUTES LATER, sneakers firmly tied on my feet, I left Darcie's Doughnuts with a box of doughnuts. I'd checked with Uncle Chris, and Maribel had never shown up at the realty with my notebook, despite saying she would. Now, what was that saying? Honey gets more bees than vinegar? I was here to see what a chocolate eclair could accomplish.

I drove to Charlie Booker's duplex and turned into his driveway, causing the forgotten dog collar to slide across the dash. First things first, and my excuse for why I was showing up again. I had to take down the for-sale sign and reclaim our giant flamingo statue. If Maribel still wanted to sell the home, we'd have to start fresh.

After tucking the sign and bird inside my trunk, I grabbed the doughnuts and hurried up to knock on the door. Nervously, I shifted the box in my arm. My hand might have been slightly sticky from sampling one on the way over. It was an old-fashioned glazed—anyone could understand that temptation.

Today there was a car in the driveway, so I had high hopes she was home. I stiffened. Well, someone was home and I could hear the conversation clearly through the door.

"That snoopy lady's back. You know, the one with the mother in jail?"

The door opened, and a man appearing to be in his early thirties blinked in the sunshine.

Flushing with cold anger that they'd been reading my notebook, I could barely speak.

"Well?" he finally said.

I eased out a breath between clenched teeth. I just needed to swallow my pride and get my book back. "Hey, my name is Stella O'Neil. I was the real estate agent for this place. I left my notebook, and Maribel said it was in your car?"

"What?" He squinted.

Was he honestly going to pretend like he didn't know what I was talking about? After what I'd just heard? "A notebook. It was left in your car?"

"There was nothing in the car."

My fingers on the doughnut box squeezed hard enough to leave dents. "Oh, Maribel said it was in there. It's a softbound notebook, kind of like a spiral. It's purple?" I tacked on the last descriptor hopefully.

"Mm. Just a second." He disappeared inside, shutting the door behind him.

I blinked at the closed door.

"She says she wants her notebook. What do I do? Just give it to her?"

I heard a woman yell, "Do whatever it takes to get her out of here. We don't need her meddling around anymore."

The door opened again and the man shoved the notebook through. "This must be it."

I snatched it up like it was a million dollar check. Fury boiling inside me stole my words.

He tipped his head, looking a little insecure. "Uh. Is that all?"

I glanced at the box of doughnuts and said, "These are for you," before thrusting it into his hands.

He took it in confusion. "Bye," he said, one eyebrow up.

I clenched my empty hand into a tight fist as I walked away. Why'd I give him the doughnuts? Frustrated, I got in my car. I tried to console myself that I didn't need to eat them, but honestly, I would have rather thrown them away instead.

I glared at him as he watched me pull out of his driveway. Someone else was watching as well, the weird neighbor.

I didn't care. Thinking some very choice words, I was ready to shake the dust from my feet and never come back.

10

At the stop sign, I opened the notebook to the first page. I was shaking, I was so angry that they'd read it, my poem, my thoughts, my memories. This was my mom, my secret. The only little bit I'd ever had of her, and I didn't want to share. It felt stolen from me again.

Deep breath. It's okay. You'll never see them again. I stared at my mom's name—recording the first time I'd ever written it. Underneath that was the state and year in which she was arrested.

And a tear stain.

I wanted to tear the page out and crumple it that someone had read my private moment.

Stop the drama. I have it back now. I read her name again. Vani Stevens. Vani short for Vanessa.

Vanessa. It was unbelievable that, at nearly thirty years old, I'd finally learned my mother's name. So far, I hadn't searched her up. I knew I was being a chicken. I knew it. There was only so much my brain could process, or maybe it was my heart. Either way, I felt like I was a balloon that had been filled with too much air and was on the very edge of popping.

I had no idea why she hadn't looked for me. I'd never received any emails, phone calls or letters. But what if I had? Was it possible that Dad destroyed her letters?

I needed to vent, and I knew just where to go.

But first I went home where, after a moment of feeling silly, I hid my notebook inside the carved rose box where I kept my great-great grandma's letters. Then I changed into my athletic gear.

I drove straight for Pump Gym where I headed for the treadmill like a mouse chasing cheese.

Like usual, the gym smelled like sweat and cinnamon essential oil that they used as a cleaning spray. I barely took any time to warm up, and soon ran like my life depended on it. My feet beat against the treadmill's belt, keeping time to my internal chant. *She's alive. Vani Stevens. She's alive.*

The real question now was what was I going to do about it? Was I ready to contact her?

I punched the speed up even further.

"Wow! You're really cooking!" said a deep voice to my right.

I jerked my gaze over and nearly fell as I lost balance. It was Robbie, the gym owner.

"H-hi," I panted, grabbing on to the side arm.

He looked like he'd been working out himself, with his sweaty hair and equally sweaty t-shirt. "I won't disturb you. I've just never seen you take the treadmill so hard before."

I stabbed the speed button to slow it down so I could hear him over the whirr of the machine.

Robbie was on the short side and muscley. He'd been a great friend to me ever since I joined the gym, one of my first in Brookfield, outside of Kari. He gave me an easy smile now. "You training for a marathon?" he asked, his dark eyebrows creasing upward.

"No. Just have some stuff I'm trying to work out. "

"Ahh. A therapeutic run. Everything okay?"

I'd slowed down now to a fast walk. Unexpectedly, I was teary. Something about the way he asked hit me in a vulnerable way.

He noticed my expression. "Aww, come on. Stretch it out and then let's go grab a water." He indicated the back room with a nod of his head.

I couldn't respond, my throat now dry and raw. Man, I was sure sick of feeling like a blubbery mess. I turned the machine off and started to stretch my quads.

He grabbed a towel and spray from one of the buckets on the floor. "Let me clean this off for you." He sprayed the handles and controls while I continued stretching. It was the thought of Maribel having read my notebook that sent me over the edge. As determined as I was to stay strong, a hot tear still slid down my cheek. Angrily, I swiped it away. As usual, Robbie was amazing and pretended he didn't notice.

Well, if I couldn't get this reigned in, he'd notice all right.

I took a swig of my water bottle, hoping to quench the emotion inside. He tossed the towel in a bucket and sauntered off. I followed.

"You're going to think I'm a basket case if I tell you," I warned as we went into his office.

"Try me," he said, perching on the edge of his desk. He should have smelled sweaty. Instead, his scent was clean with a hint of spice.

I chose the chair in the corner. Hesitantly, with a lot of

stutters and pauses, I filled him in with discovering that my long absent mom was still alive. "I have her name now. So I guess I could try to track her down."

"Have you done it yet?"

I shook my head, and redid my own sweaty ponytail. "I just don't think I can. I'm such a chicken."

"Let me help, then." His voice was encouraging like when he was trying to get me to do another leg press. "Investigating's practically a gift of mine."

"You're an expert on investigating?" I said, skeptically.

"Yeah! Sure!" His confident expression might have fooled me if not for the worried expression tightening around his eyes. "But first, maybe we need some energy." He sprang up in an obvious sign that he did not need energy and disappeared into the walk-in closet. I heard rattling. A second later he returned with two protein drinks.

"One for you, one for me. It's good for the brain."

"What exactly are you saying?" I teased.

"What? No. I mean good for my brain. Yours is good already."

Poor guy was falling all over himself. I let him off the hook. "I probably need it. I've been pretty drained this week, and I'm just getting back to normal if you can call it that."

He grabbed the back of my chair and wheeled it behind his desk, and then sat beside me. After a flourish of cracking his knuckles, he slid the keyboard closer and began to hen-peck until a search engine popped up on the screen.

"What's her name?" he asked.

My mouth dropped open. Until this moment I'd never told another soul my mother's name. I'd never verbally identified myself as her daughter. Heat crept up into my cheeks.

"Vanessa Stevens is my mother. Vani for short." I said. The words made me slightly dizzy and at the same time, oddly freeing. I drew in a deep breath.

Wow. Something had changed, and I felt different. I'd have to dwell on that more later. Right now, my muscles started tightening again, as I realized I was about to see what the results would bring up.

He typed it in, his fingers painfully slow. It was like watching a steam roller on its lowest gear about to run over a car. I couldn't look away.

When he finished, his finger hovered over the enter button. "You ready?" he asked, his eyebrows crinkling together.

I nodded. "Yeah."

He studied me for a second and then glanced over at the still-open office door. I could see him calculating what he would do if I lost it.

"I promise. I won't freak out." Gently I laid my hand over his finger, and together, we pressed the key.

The button whirled its rainbow. My heart thumped.

Robbie reached over and squeezed my shoulder. "Relax. Whatever it says, you can handle it. You're strong enough. This is just to answer a few questions. It doesn't force you into any action."

Gratefulness rose inside my heart. It was true, wasn't it? Here I was, mentally already ten steps ahead, trying to figure out if this meant I had to contact her, and how I was going to do that.

I took another deep breath and tried to force my muscles to unknot. The air left me in a huff.

Something had come up.

His hand paused in mid-squeeze. We both leaned in to read.

"Vanessa O'Neil at Ashmount Women's Penitentiary was denied probation for the murder of FBI agent Geralds. Her next opportunity is in one year," Robbie read.

It was the first time I really learned her crime. I'd known it was bad from what Uncle Chris had started to say before I'd run from the restaurant that day. There was a picture. A very sad, thin woman with brown hair stared into the camera. Her lips were parted slightly as if she wanted to protest, but the lines around her eyes showed a resignation as if she realized no one would listen.

"You have the same color of eyes," Robbie noted.

"What?" I was numb.

"Your eyes, look." He pointed.

Hers were blue. Like mine.

I sat back. All these years I'd stared at my reflection in the mirror. Put mascara on. Plucked my eyebrows. Picked at my face. Those eyes, her eyes, were looking back at me.

A lump grew in my throat, and her picture blurred.

"You okay?" Robbie asked.

He was being so kind, too kind.

I nodded, unable to speak.

"Aww," he wrapped his arms around me and pulled me into a hug. I lay against his chest, muscular and firm, and listened to his heart thump. His warmth and strength comforted me. I couldn't speak, just pressed my lips together to control the tears.

I will be okay. I will be okay. I will always be okay.

"Looks like she's up for parole again," he murmured. One of his arms moved, and I heard the keys click. I peeked out to see what he was doing. "There's more about her crime here, if you want to read about it."

"I know about it," I said, hiding my face again.

"She was young when she got arrested. Wow. Super young."

I peeked again. I had no idea how old she was. Robbie pointed to her date of birth and I realized she was only twenty years older than me. That made her younger than I was by a year when she got arrested.

I sat back and tried to understand that. To be my age...been married for six years, had a five-year-old daughter...to leave that all behind. To spend the rest of my life behind bars.

Addiction was a brutal thing. So brutal it had led to murder.

Robbie continued to rub my shoulders with soft circles. "You doing okay?"

I nodded. "Thank you so much. I don't think I could have done that alone."

"Hey, I'm glad I could be here for you. Any time you need me, you just ask. I mean that."

I read the rest of the link and sighed. There was no mention of me. But why would there be? Who mentions the children that were left behind? It wasn't a funeral announcement, even though it felt like a death.

"I think I need to go run again," I said.

Before I left, I searched the same web address up on my phone and saved it so that I could read it more thoroughly in private.

"Yeah, of course." Awkwardly, he stood up. As I followed, he leaned down and cleared the information from his computer. Then he ran his hand through his short hair. "Running is probably just the thing for you. Don't forget to stay hydrated. Seriously. Stress and anxiety can do a number on you."

I nodded. Grabbing my water, I went to run my demons away again.

11

*R*obbie probably thought I was going to run on the treadmill again. Not this time. I needed a change of scenery and some space away from people.

I backed out of the parking space and turned onto the road, making the dog collar slide across the dash with a rattle. Oh, yeah. I'd forgotten about that. I wonder if I still could find out who it belonged to. Someone had to know something about it.

I drove to my house and grabbed my pepper spray. This time I was going the opposite way than I normally ran. I wanted to explore where the other end of the road led.

My legs were pretty weary and feeling a little noodle-like from my earlier run. I stretched them a bit and took it slow. First I passed a little farmhouse that was my neighbor. They seemed to be gone at work all the time and I hadn't met them yet, although their cat had been a visitor many times. Then the farmland started up again, fields tilled to reveal dark brown dirt. I breathed in deeply and savored the rich scent of earth.

One field shimmered with green sprouts, so pale that when you looked directly for them, all you saw was dirt. But as I ran, the sheen was visible like the palest green in a rainbow.

My feet and lungs and arms all moved rhythmically in their pounding. My blood coursing, my cheeks burning slightly from the cold. I loved it.

I always thought I was someone who could face challenges head on. All this news about my mom had shaken me so much that, looking back, I didn't think I would have been brave enough to have met with Uncle Chris had I known this was what he would say. However, the experience also showed me that I could get back up when things in life knocked me down. I was strong enough, and I was going to draw on that strength to put these pieces of my family back together.

The field next to me narrowed as the trees and river came closer to the road. I jogged around a curve to see a bridge to be crossed. It wasn't especially noteworthy, just a dirt road edged by concrete barriers on both sides. Yet the water running underneath called to me, and I decided I wanted to explore it.

Carefully, I picked my way between the overgrown grass and bushes down the side of the bridge into the culvert below. The clear water gurgled as it rushed by. I perched on a boulder and watched little bits of shadows mixed with dapples of sunlight dance across its surface.

This was a place that felt untouched by humans. I shivered with a childlike excitement of finding my own special undiscovered hide-away. My muscles protested as I stood again. I walked down the bank, the river slowing and widening the further I went. I figured I must be behind the farmland by now, although it was still heavily wooded around me. Through the trees, I caught what I thought was a glimpse of a brown field.

Another dozen steps and I froze in my tracks. I saw brown alright, but it wasn't the dirt field. Instead, it was tons and tons of shipping boxes that lay in tangled piles throughout the bushes. I glanced around. Call me paranoid, but all those Cold Case mystery TV shows had me freaked out at finding the unexpected.

My nosy side pushed me forward to investigate, the pepper spray in hand just in case. Now I saw the reason why the water had slowed down. The boxes were damming it up. Why were they here?

The area around them was thick with undergrowth. I didn't see any way to this point except the way I'd just come. No, my guess was that someone must have dumped them off up stream. After the winter snow melted, the water had brought them down here.

Where did they come from initially?

A crack came from the brush to my right. I ducked and froze. I'd done it again, hadn't I? Stumbled into something with no way out.

My breath squeezed against my chest as I held it. Quietly, I watched. Nothing more moved. Then, nearly causing me to scream, a bird rushed from the undergrowth up into the trees. It perched on a branch and tipped its head, its bead-eye focused on me. His yellow beak opened as he let out a scolding chirp.

My breath hissed between my clenched teeth. It was me that was the intruder, scaring the bird. I glanced around again to be sure I was alone, and then carefully picked my way through the swampy grass to the closest boxes.

There were address labels on them, all different addresses.

That's all I needed to see. I fished my phone from my pocket, snapped a few pictures, and then dialed 911.

"911. What are you reporting?" asked a very nonemotional woman.

"This is a nonemergency. I think I just came up on a stash of stolen mail."

"Where are you located?"

"I'm at the back side of the Johnson road. A little ways under the bridge to the right."

"We'll send an officer to investigate."

With that, she hung up. Great. Now, what was I supposed to do? Stay here and wait? Leave and hope the cops found it okay?

I decided to poke through the boxes a bit to see what was there. One of them had split open and dog food spilled out. However, most appeared empty with package chips floating about.

All right, what's really going on here? Was this what Carlson was referring to the other day?

Sirens in the distance made me pause for a second until I realized they must be for something else. The cops wouldn't have sirens on to meet me here.

I hit the browser button on my phone. One second later, I sucked in my breath. The last thing I'd searched for was Vani O'Neil and there she was staring sadly at me in her bail hearing photo. A lump grew in my throat. I zoomed in for a second, swallowing hard. Those eyes, brilliantly clear blue, just like two robin eggs stared back at me. Just like mine. It was dismal to think of all the things I'd forgotten about her.

I sighed and closed the web page, before reopening another one. Jabbing with my thumbs, I typed in *delivery truck crime* and the date of the post office stamp on the box closest to me.

A page of options popped up. The first five were all the same story. I clicked one.

DELIVERY TRUCKS BEING HIT *over the last year.*

At least six known attacks have been perpetrated against ATX delivery services in the last year. The trucks are found empty, with the drivers bound and gagged. In each case, the truck has been taken off of its delivery route and forced into isolated situations. One was found under a bridge. The other, in an alley. Several more were found sitting on rarely used county service roads. In each case, the thieves wore masks and voice disguisers, making a clean get-away. Police believe there is one off-site boss—a ring leader—who organizes each hit. No leads are coming from the crimes at this time.

CREEPY-CRAWLIES RAN DOWN MY BACK, and I swatted at them, not knowing if it was a bug, or if I was just nervous about being isolated in the middle of the woods with what might be a ton of evidence. With my luck, this would be the one in a million time that the bad guys decided to come back.

I shook my head. This wasn't their dumping spot. It made perfect sense to me that the police would investigate upstream to find the original spot where these had been abandoned.

The sound of crunching leaves turned my muscles into ivory. Dear heavens, why was I standing out in the open? What if it was the thieves after all? I spun around desperately and finally hid behind a skinny tree. I might have laughed at how ridiculous I looked—like a fat cat hiding behind a few blades of grass—if I hadn't been so terrified.

Luckily, it was two police officers. "Hello!" one of them called.

"Hi, I'm here," I said, waving a hand.

They walked toward me and one of them whistled. "What's all this you found?"

I explained the story of how I ended up down here. As they started to examine the boxes I tried to blend into the background. I wanted to eavesdrop a bit.

"You think this is from that delivery truck jacking?" said the first officer.

"It fits."

"Most of these are filled with junk," he said, nudging what looked like a hairdryer that had spilled out of a box.

"They dumped off the stuff that wasn't valuable."

Of course, I took that moment to step back, nearly falling as a stick rolled under my foot. My girlie squeal didn't help my ninja stealth skills any.

They both looked over. The second officer came over and took a statement from me. Then, without further ado, they dismissed me like an annoying mosquito from their crime scene.

My walk home wasn't nearly so fun. Once back at the house, I made myself a sandwich and searched for the news story about the delivery truck robberies again. Elbows against the kitchen counter, I scrolled slowly. There was something I'd read the first time that stood out. Ah. There it was. Taking a chomp from my sandwich, I clicked to reread it.

It was in the second to the final line... the ring leader.

My brain went to the other place where I'd seen a lot of boxes. A wall of boxes, to be exact. Charlie Booker's house. And hadn't his neighbor, Marge, mentioned that there was a revolving train of people going in and out of there?

I chewed some more before searching for the article about the thieves that were busted for Charlie's death. The search pulled up the same mugshots. This time, however, the search engine also brought up another item that featured a candid photo of the group of men outside the house where they'd been arrested.

There was even a video. I clicked it and watched as the police led the handcuffed young men to the van. Seeing the four of them stand next to the other officers, I could see the thieves were all on the shorter side, maybe my height.

I replayed the footage. Something about it really bothered me.

A knock pounded on my door. I leaned away from the counter, listening. I wasn't expecting anyone, that's for sure. Was it the police with more questions about the boxes under the bridge? Could it be Richie? Maybe there was something wrong with his mom.

I brushed the crumbs off my shirt and walked down the hall to the living room. Trying to be discreet, I peeked out the side window. There was an unfamiliar white van parked in my driveway. Was it a delivery company?

I was straining to see more when I heard a yap. An unmistakably small-dog-excited-to-see-me yap. I'd recognize it anywhere.

Peanut.

I froze, afraid to go open the door and confirm who I knew was waiting there.

"Stella! I know you're mad at me. Please, let me in."

Taking a big breath, I walked over and wrenched the door open. I wasn't in the mood to hide my anger. This was ultimately the man who was responsible for my mom being in prison. For deceiving me.

I glared at my grandfather, and he stared back through his thick glasses. Peanut trembled in his arms, eager to get down and give me a thousand licks of welcome. She barked to get my attention.

I wanted to shut the door and run away, and at the same time wanted to swoop Peanut up and bury my face in her soft fur.

What caught me off guard was the expression of fear on Oscar's whiskered face. My breath caught in my throat in a hiccup.

"What?" I finally gasped.

He stared up at me sadly, his normally stern, grumpy wrinkles folding into an expression of misery.

Of loss.

It hurt to see it. I had to drop my gaze to the floor as tears pricked my eyes. I cleared my throat and started again. "What do you want, Oscar?"

"It's good to see you, Stella. So good." His raspy voice sounded like he'd been gargling barbed wire. Peanut barked again to remind me not to forget about her.

I stood there, swaying in the mixture of emotions. What he did to me. Yet he was the first family I'd connected with that had made me feel safe. My long lost heritage finally found in him.

"Stella, may I come in?"

Like a robot, I backed away from the door. He shuffled inside and set Peanut on the floor. She immediately jumped on my legs, her sharp nails scrabbling against my shins.

I picked her up and smothered my face into her fur even as her head wiggled to give me a few licks.

Oscar glanced around the entryway, taking in the flooring boxes. His eyes dropped to the floor that I'd already laid it.

"Why are you here?" I asked.

His nostrils widened with a heavy sigh. "Your Uncle called me."

"Uncle Chris?" Shock reverberated through me.

His white head bobbed. "Nearly twenty years since I'd last

heard from that boy and first thing out of his mouth is how I screwed up again."

Well, that was interesting. And so true. Still, my dad and Uncle Chris had played a big part in the coverup. "You aren't alone. It must be a family trait," I mumbled into Peanut's neck.

"Yeah. Well, honey. We're a bunch of screw-ups. One thing I can tell you, God sure does have a way of bringing beauty from ashes because, after everything we did, we still got you."

A wave of regret washed over me. I was so sad to be here, like this, with him.

"You want to sit down?" I asked.

"It seems like the best way to answer any questions you might have."

I turned toward the living room, skirting around a pile of laminate floor pieces. His shuffling steps proved he was making his way slowly behind me.

I chose my favorite couch under the window and settled Peanut on my lap. She immediately lay down with her nose pointing off my legs. Like taking sips of hot chamomile tea, stroking her warm fur did a world of good in calming me.

Oscar studied the couch that sagged in the center.

"My desk chair is over there, if that would be better," I offered.

He nodded and grabbed it with swollen hands. He slowly dragged it over on its wheels and eased himself down with a heavy sigh. His gaze rested on me, sharper now, and suddenly I felt that profiler's stare of a former FBI agent.

"What? I didn't do anything," I said rather hotly.

"I know. It's me. I'm wondering what it is you want to hear."

"How about the truth." Peanut looked back at me at my tone. I rubbed her ears to soothe her.

"You sure you want to know?"

"I know what Uncle Chris told me."

"He doesn't know everything. Maybe not even enough. Stella, I've been working all these years to get your mom out of prison."

His words stunned me. "You think she's innocent?" Anger started to bubble inside. Why would he have arrested her then?

"The FBI agent she killed was crooked."

"So why did she get arrested then?"

"I saved her life. I wasn't supposed to be there that night, so it shocked everyone when I showed up. The other arresting officer was going to kill her, and if I hadn't been there, he would have done it. To save her, I put Vani under arrest. They wanted to take her to jail to process her. I insisted on coming along so nothing bad would happen to her. There was a long string of hand-in-hand workings with the FBI and the drug dealers. Your mom was at the wrong place at the wrong time."

"Uncle Chris brought her there."

He sighed. "Addiction is a horrible thing. I didn't know the trouble Chris was in. It was my fault, always being away at work. He's never forgiven himself for what happened. It knocked him straight into rehab, and he's been clean ever since, for which I'm grateful. He doesn't know about the crooked cop. I couldn't risk telling him or your father. I didn't know who else was crooked on my surveillance team. If the wrong person knew that I knew about them being rogue, all of our lives would have been in danger."

"What have you tried to do to help her?"

"I've tried to get her out. So far, I've been blocked from every one of her parole hearings. She's about to have another one in a few months. I've paid for an attorney to fight her case."

"Well, it doesn't seem like it's been working."

"It has. She originally was looking at the death penalty. He was able to plea that down to a crime that would one day be eligible for parole. We're hoping that this next time she comes up for it, she will get it."

"Why didn't anyone tell me about her?"

"I had no idea you didn't know about your mother, Stella. The day after your mom was arrested, your dad swooped you away to Seattle. Honestly, I didn't fight his decision to have no contact with me. I figured the more distance between us, the safer you'd be. When you came back," he opened his hands, palm up. "You gave no indication that you didn't know about Vani. I was so overwhelmed that you still wanted to meet me."

Those darn tears were coming again. Blinking hard, I stared at Peanut, watching as she blurred into a yellow love blob. I wanted everything to be okay between us, yet I didn't trust him yet.

He seemed to sense my indecision and uneasily stood on legs that acted like two wobbly bowling pins. "I'm going now. You come by the house if you have any more questions."

"Wait. You're leaving? How did you get here?"

He jerked his thumb in the driveway's direction. "Georgie, my girlfriend's employee, brought me. She thinks that I'm dropping off some home-cooked spaghetti.

Spaghetti. He remembered my comfort food. My forehead wrinkled. "But you're not carrying anything."

"I left it on the porch. Help me with it now."

I followed him to the door and opened it to see a white van idling out in the driveway. A young woman close to my age glanced up from the driver's seat and waved. A handful of air fresheners hung off the rear-view mirror.

"There's your spaghetti. And that's Georgie." He pointed one crooked finger at a towel-covered pot on the porch step. He eyed me. "You want to meet her?"

In a flux between auto-drive and ingrained manners, I wandered after him, still holding the dog.

The woman unrolled her window as we approached. "Hi, there." Her voice was cheery.

"Georgie, this is my granddaughter, Stella. Stella, this is Georgie Tanner."

I smiled back. "Nice to meet you."

"Nice to meet you as well! I see you have the infamous Peanut."

The dog wiggled in my arms to get to her, sending a tiny flash of jealousy through me. She reached out to scratch the dog's chin, even as Oscar harrumphed.

"I mean Bear, don't I? Don't I, you little dumpling?" she cooed at the dog. Then she winked at me. "I do like to yank Oscar's chain every once and again," she whispered.

"I'm standing right here." He scowled.

Georgie laughed. "Well, come on. You know I have to go pick up those tourists from the diner." And then she added to me, "I'm a tour guide for the Baker Street Bed and Breakfast. I don't know if you're a morning person, but if you'd ever like to grab a cup of coffee, feel free to stop by the b&b. Us new people have to unite." She grinned. "Especially since we both know Oscar. I'm sure we have lots to talk about!"

I had to smile at that, while Oscar grumbled something about "disrespectful young pups." Nevertheless, I saw a glimmer of amusement in his eyes.

"Sounds great." I said. "Maybe one day on my way to the realty office."

"Oh the Flamingo realty! My good friend Kari works there."

That's right. I do seem to recall Kari mentioning something about having a friend named Georgie. "I think she wanted to introduce us."

Georgie laughed. "She's going to flip that I circumvented her. We'll have to plan a girl's night out or something."

"That sounds like fun."

Oscar was walking to the passenger side. I followed, still carrying Peanut.

As he climbed into the van, he said, "Good job with the floor. I'd say I was impressed, but you have a spirit of steel. I know you'll accomplish whatever you put your mind to."

I handed him the little dog, reluctantly. "Thanks, Oscar."

And maybe I meant it in more ways than one.

13

I picked up the spaghetti pot as I headed back in the house. Now that the metaphorical band-aid had been ripped off, so to speak, I felt a bit stronger. I was ready to dig in more about my mom.

I placed the pot in the refrigerator and refilled a water bottle then went back to grab my laptop. I sat with my feet propped on one side of my broken-down couch, making the springs squeal, and typed her name. This time, I felt only a slight shock at seeing her again. I zoomed in. Prison had been hard, I could see that. However, there was a softness to her that remained—there in the curve of her lip, the pink in her cheeks. The way her eyes seemed to hold a smile.

It was a little disconcerting. It was as if her expression were acting like a liquidified key, unlocking memories I'd forgotten

123

I had. There was the time I draped my blanky around my shoulders and ran through the kitchen declaring I was 'Fat Man.' I remember seeing her eyes smile in the same way, even though her face stayed ever so serious as she announced I was the best 'Fat Man' she'd ever seen.

I typed in the prison website and searched for the directions to communicate with an inmate. I took a screenshot of the address and rules with my phone, and then shut the laptop.

I leaned back with my hands folded behind my neck and stared out into the back yard. What should my letter say to her?

That question opened the floodgates of words which turned into nonsensical mush with no clear direction. I rubbed my forehead, feeling overwhelmed, before deciding to turn to a trick I'd learned long ago to help process.

I walked over to my wood carved chest and pulled out my purple notebook.

After opening to a blank page, I started in the center of the paper and wrote one word. Mom. After that, I wrote the next thing that popped into my head, and then the next, carefully shaping the words into a spiral shape around the first word. As more words came, my spiral expanded. Thoughts like, "Soft, tears, loss, beautiful. Nutcracker, stories, miss you.

I wrote and wrote, until my words threatened to spill off the edge of the paper. I flipped it over and started on the other side. So many words. Some were angry. Some were confused.

Most spoke of the empty hole she'd left.

When I finished, I lay back against the arm of the couch, the storm inside spent. I was surprised to see it was dark out. I'd been so lost in my own emotions I hadn't noticed the passing of time.

I stretched a bit, and then walked to the kitchen to refill my water bottle. After a sip, I headed out to the back porch, snagging a cookie on the way. The swing was calling me this night.

I sat on it and stared up at the stars. Stars that seemed to whisper, "Yes, you can ignore us by shutting yourself in your house. But that's a delusion. You're only a speck in time, while we are nearly forever."

The knowledge that the vastness of the black space stitching them together actually went on for millions of light years overwhelmed me. I shuddered and turned my face away, once again the loser of this strange game of chicken. They would beat me every time.

Gazing straight ahead was a relief. Trees stood firm in the shadows, as if stating, "This is here and now. We aren't going anywhere. You can touch us. We have history and strength. We are dependable."

The chirping of the frogs was loud tonight, coming from the creek that ran past Richie's house. I thought about Richie's mom, Truly, and her sweet smile even when her body failed her at times. There was a peace there.

My thoughts skipped toward Richie. He was like one of these trees. There was a security in him, in the curve of his muscles under his shirt, the shape of his hands, calloused, but nimble and strong. His eyes sparkled with cleverness, and he always had a deep thoughtfulness that was the undercurrent of our interactions, even the few awkward moments we had. It was almost as if he were weighing me, and not in the way I'd been judged by men before. Oh, sure. I've no doubt he'd noticed my hair, eyes, and other, ahem, body aspects. I'd once been a track star, and I was pretty proud of the booty it had shaped. But with him, it was different. He studied me like he was curious about what I thought. I wondered if I measured up to his expectations.

I snorted. He probably thought I was a hot mess. Sometimes it felt like everybody around me had this crazy life already figured out.

Not me, though. I had so many loose ends. So many ways to feel lost. Maybe that's why I didn't like looking at the night sky. It reminded me of how out of control life really was.

My toe scuffed over and over again against the wood planks as

I closed my eyes. The rhythm lulled me as I gently pushed the swing. Rocking me. Like a mothers's arms. Soothing me.

I swung a few more times but the comfortable feeling faded. My eyes fluttered open, and I gazed at the trees again, even as my foot dragged the swing to a stop. I didn't want to be rocked by a placebo mom. I wanted the real thing, something I'd never had before, that had always been denied to me. I wasn't sure what was stable and strong anymore.

Maybe it was the stars after all.

Interrupting my thoughts was the crack of my car door slamming shut in the front yard.

14

I scrambled through the side gate and into the front yard. A car screeched down the road, leaving me gasping and staring after it from the end of my driveway. There were no identifying marks other than two red tail lights.

They were trying to break into my car! I stomped over to my car fuming mad. Everything appeared normal on the outside. I yanked the door open and stuck my head inside. There were no ripped ignition wires like I'd expected. Relief rushed through me. I was about to congratulate myself on thwarting a car robbery when I realized, it was the sound of the car door *shutting* that had alerted me to their presence in the first place.

Which meant that whatever they had come for, they had accomplished.

I reached into the door pocket for the emergency flashlight I kept there and clicked it on. The beam shone white against the seats. Leaning in, I moved it to shine in the back. Now, I have to admit, I was kind of a neat freak when it came to my car. Many years with Dad had drilled into me that keeping things clean meant I appreciated what I had. So nothing seemed out of place. However, there wasn't a lot there to look like it could be out of place to begin with.

It was as I ducked to look under the seats that Carlson's statement about finding a car bomb in the trunk of the thieves waltzed out of my memory banks with a big ol' hello. I jumped back, nearly losing the flashlight in a juggling match with my panicked hands. What if they had booby-trapped the car with a bomb?

I back-pedaled a few more steps, trying to judge what would be a safe distance away from a possible explosion. I dropped to my knees and swept the beam under the car. I didn't see anything, but what was I looking for, anyway? A bunch of wires? Something that looked like a giant firecracker? I walked around the back of the car and checked the other side.

Nothing stood out to me.

I flashed the light along the driveway. There was some

crushed grass that could have been made by the intruder. Then again, it could have been from me when I checked the mailbox earlier.

What do I do? Text Carlson? I wrinkled my nose, imagining how that conversation would go down. Something like, "Hey... what are you doing? Can you come out here and check my car? I think someone rigged it with a car bomb."

Ridiculous. I could almost hear the snort he'd be sure to give. No, the best bet was just to lock the car up and wait until morning.

I grabbed my keys from inside and pointed them at the car. My thumb hovered over the lock button. As I delayed, my inner voice questioned, "If it's so ridiculous, why don't you hit the door lock?" It was rather rudely answered with a vision of me putting the key into the ignition the next morning to start it, followed by a cartoon-size explosion. I shuddered and went to get my phone. Let him snort. He did say he wondered if they had found all the pipe bombs, and now I was freaked out.

Still, I was going to play it somewhat cool. Instead of calling, I'd just text. It seemed less dramatic that way. —**Hey, hope I'm not bothering you. Not sure of what to do. Someone broke into my car.** My thumb hovered over the send button, wondering if what I'd said was urgent enough, and then I added—**I think they tampered with it.**

There. Not quite so hysterical as a bomb, yet urgent enough. Congratulating myself on my excellent communications skills, I hit send and gave the car another uneasy look before heading inside the house.

Of course, here in the dark foyer, my imagination jumped into overdrive. Had the car that had raced down the street left someone behind? What if that person had snuck into the house while I was distracted outside?

A creak came from one of the upstairs bedrooms. Cold goosebumps jumped all over my body. I checked my texts. Carlson hadn't answered. In fact, it showed that he hadn't even read it yet.

I stared upstairs, the stairwell dark and gloomy. The wind picked up and rushed through the trees outside. Another squeak came from upstairs. Was it just the old house settling? Maybe I should call 911. They could send some anonymous guy. It wouldn't matter if he thought I was crazy and overreacting. I grimaced. Too late! Why I hadn't I done that in the first time instead of jumping to contact Carlson?

I knew why. Panic. And panic was about to make another decision for me. I sent a text to Richie.

—You around? I have a weird situation at the house.

My hand was trembling as I lowered the phone. Wow, I was majorly keyed up. Okay, calm yourself down. Think about puppies and kittens.

I walked over to the hall lamp to turn it on, adrenaline keeping my steps light. A squeal on the kitchen floorboards made every one of my muscles freeze. I knew it! Someone *had* snuck in while I was examining the car! Heart pounding, I backed up to the wall. My eyes strained to see into the shadowy darkness, only illuminated by the light I'd left on in the kitchen.

I *had* left a light on, right? Or was it another person who'd turned it on?

Weapon. Weapon. Where was a weapon?

And why was no one answering my messages?

I quietly slid along the wall, listening hard. The problem with listening hard mixed with adrenaline was all I could hear was the swooshing of my pulse in my ears. Were they watching me right now? Waiting to see what I would do? I traveled toward the door, ready to scream at the slightest movement. I didn't know what good a scream would do, however now was not the time to be questioning any defensive measures. Now was the time to escape.

A bright light blazed against the hallway railing, and I made good on my threat to scream. A second later, I realized it was car headlights. I scrambled to the door, ready to open it until I stopped dead in my tracks.

I didn't know if the bad guys had returned.

A cowboy hat silhouetted in truck lights sealed the deal. It was Richie.

I wrenched open the door and ran down the stairs. "Richie! Thank you so much for showing up! Someone broke into my car!" In a babble, I told him about my fears about the bomb. Then, to make things extra confusing, out came the information about the weird letter I'd received earlier.

"Whoa? What's going on?" He walked around my car carefully before coming and pulling me into his arms. "You're shaking. Calm down. It's going to be okay."

More headlights came down the road, illuminating Richie and I. This time, I recognized Carlson's cop car. He got out, slamming his door. "What's going on here? Take your hands off of her!"

I saw his hand drop to his holster and called out, "Carlson, no. It's not Richie. I had to call him when I didn't think you were coming."

He scowled. "Of course I'd come. Check your phone."

My hands were still trembling. I read my messages to see he'd texted me back. **—On my way.**

"Oh, so you called him first. Maybe I should go," said Richie.

"No, thank you for coming. Both of you." I swiveled between them, trying to look them both in the eye. Quickly, I told the story of hearing my car door slam and seeing the car speed away.

"I wasn't sure if it was a bomb. You know, after we talked." I blew out my cheeks, feeling foolish. "And then I heard creaking in the house...." I let the thought hang. Nothing was going to rescue this.

In just a second, Richie had my engine hood up and was examining everything inside. "Don't worry. I know cars like the back of my hand. I'll have this sorted out."

Carlson grunted as he lowered himself down to his knees. "I may not know car engines, but after years of dealing with IED's, I know my way around what an explosive devise looks like." He flipped over on his back, shooting the beam of a pen light up toward my gas tank.

Another gust of wind ripped through the trees. I stood with my arms wrapped around myself to stop the shivering. The two men combed over every square inch of my car. I was more embarrassed than anything when they found nothing.

Carlson climbed out from under the car. "I'll go check the house. Wait here."

"I'll help," offered Richie as he lowered the car hood.

Carlson eyed him. "I don't want to put a civilian in danger." He marched into the house.

"He's quite the guy, huh?" asked Richie, brushing off his hands as he came to stand by me.

I nodded, too nervous to answer. We stared toward the house. One by one, the windows lit up throughout the house.

About fifteen minutes later, Carlson returned. "It's all clear. My guess is that what you thought was your car door slamming was actually a backfire of the car that passed your house. Pretty typical, especially if it was speeding like you said. Still, it might be a sign to quit watching so many of those TV shows," Carlson said with a small grin.

Richie stuffed his hands into his pockets. "Hey, I'd think anyone would be freaked out. Especially after the letter she got."

"Did you ever find anything out about that?" I asked Carlson

The big dude nodded. "We tracked down the letters to a magazine that was distributed to the discount store in our town."

"Wow, how on earth could you know that?" I was impressed.

"There's a color code at the bottom of one of the letters. Using it, we discovered where it had been printed and where that batch had been sent."

"Seems like if you knew where it was purchased, you could find the person who bought it pretty quick. What with security camera's and all." Richie's jaw muscle jumped under his skin.

Carlson eased back, his leather boots squeaking. They eyed each other.

Wait... what was this? Were they sizing each other up? Suddenly, I felt like I wasn't even in the driveway.

"Sorry for bothering you both," I said, hoping to break their silent showdown. "I'm glad you both showed up, though, too much TV or not."

That seemed to work. Carlson turned toward me and his face transformed into a grin that nearly made me gasp. Had I ever seen him smile like that before? It was almost...charismatic. "Any time, Stella. Seriously. It's why I chose to wear the uniform." He nodded nobly at me.

"No need to bother the officer," Richie butted in. "I'm just down the road. You know I can be here in a heartbeat, day or night."

"As can I," added Carlson.

"I'm closer," said Richie through a smile full of gritted teeth.

Carlson nodded patronizingly. "I carry a gun."

"Who says I don't?"

"Mine's bigger." Carlson patted his pistol.

Whoa, now. I didn't want to hear any more about anyone's big guns. Who knew what they'd be comparing next.

"So, anyway," I said in near frenzied cheeriness. "It's late and all. I'm going to head inside. I'll definitely keep it in mind if I run into more trouble. Usually, I can take care of myself, but my nerves got to me tonight."

"It's all the stuff you've been dealing with," Carlson said, with a sympathetic expression.

Richie stared at him and then back at me. "Yeah, all that really hard stuff. Takes an emotional toll. I know how it is, you've been there so much for me and my mom."

This time, Carlson gave Richie the 'look'. He'd clearly seemed to have lost this round. Then he perked up. "Well, have a good night. Let's grab another burger again soon. That was fun the last time we went."

Oh, boy. I know how that sounded, and apparently, so did Richie. He rubbed the back of his neck, and glanced down.

Then, giving his hat a tug in my direction, Richie nodded. "I'm glad everything is okay. I'll be seeing you around, Stella." With that, he shambled toward his truck, the soles of his boots crunching the gravel.

Carlson watched him get into his truck, and then turned back to me. "Something going on between you two?" His nostrils flared as he waited for my answer.

"Nothing's going on between me or anyone," I said.

His eyebrows raised but he nodded. "You have a good night, Stella. Stay safe." He climbed into his car and followed Richie down the road.

15

I walked inside the house. Terrific. I've turned out to be the idiot who heard a backfire and immediately concocted some crazy story about my car being broken into. Heat flushed through my cheeks. Even worse, my imagination had the car rigged for a bomb, ready to blow me to bits. Not to mention how those two guys acted like strutting roosters, which irritated the heck out of me. Still, they both had a point.

Maybe my mom *was* taking a toll on me. I just needed to take the first step and get the letter written. I'd probably feel a lot better after it was finished.

Decision made, I wrote well into the night. In it, I included everything I'd ever wanted to say, every thought, ever question. After re-reading it, I tore it up and wrote a watered-down version which amounted to a weird introduction and confessing that I missed and loved her.

THE NEXT MORNING, I walked to the mailbox with the fated letter clutched tightly in my hand. I was so emotionally charged each step felt like a shock through my body. I swear even the air was electrified. And not in a good way. In a dark way that spoke of foreboding.

Danger.

I shook my head. *Don't be silly. Remember how last night you called in the troops for some car backfiring? Or how about the time you ripped off your shirt in the middle of a hike because you were convinced a spider was on you?*

I glanced up the road. Oh, boy. Here comes the mailman now. My hand was hot and sweaty. The fragile paper reminded me of how vulnerable I really was. I swallowed hard, knowing that my whole life was about to change the instant the mail carrier whisked the letter away.

The vehicle rolled up.

"Morning!" said the mailman cheerfully. "I see you have something for me." He reached toward me with a gloved hand.

I nodded and held out the envelope. It felt like it weighed twenty pounds. *Dear God, help me to let it go.* I swear I felt the sting of tears in my eyes, but I was able to let him take it without the tug-of-war I'd feared.

He grinned again, not noticing my struggle. "I have something for you, as well." He rustled through one of the plastic bins sitting next to him before pulling out a colorful sheath of papers.

Ads. Wonderful. Oh, goodie. A bill. I smiled as I accepted them, the sentiment feeling fake and plastic, and then he waved and drove away, unknowingly taking a piece of my heart in the form of pen marks scrawled on notebook paper.

I watched him disappear down the road, before slowly turning back to the house. What would happen now? Would she write me back?

It was then that I saw it. A perfect shoe track with the corkscrew print, left by someone walking straight for my house.

I sucked in a gulp of air and compared my own shoe size to it, even though it was obviously nearly twice as big. Someone had been here! That same person as the one at Charlie Booker's house. This proves it! I jogged inside the house, returning with my phone so I could take some photos.

First, I snapped a shot with my shoe next to it for reference, then I squatted down to examine it closer. What popped into my mind wasn't the size difference between my own foot, but the picture of the thieves getting arrested. Something had bothered me when I'd first seen it. I knew what it was now.

Those men had been on the shorter size, and their shoe size seemed to be in proportion.

This track here was made by a huge foot. Maybe even one that had been special ordered.

I searched all along my driveway and around my car for more tracks. Unfortunately, there was only that one print in the soft dirt by my mailbox that pointed in the direction of my driveway.

I stared at my car. So it hadn't been a backfire after all. They had gone inside it. But why?

I walked around the car again, closely examining the vehicle, hoping to find something I'd missed last night. Nothing. I opened the door and searched around. Not seeing anything, I sat inside the driver's seat. My fingers clenched the wheel as I let out a breath. It was eerie. I could almost catch a whiff of the intruder who sat here. Yet, nothing seemed out of place.

A thump against the passenger window caused me to jump. What was that? The hair on my neck stood on end until I saw the bird imprint, complete with a dusty outline of petite wing feathers, against the dirty glass. I climbed out and ran to the other side of the car.

Below the door was a little brown bird. He was alive, although stunned. His tiny feet jerked, and his chest quivered with minuscule breaths.

A slight movement to the left of me caught my attention. It was the neighbor's cat. So far, it hadn't seen the bird, being more interested in a butterfly that fluttered over a patch of buttercups. I had to act quick.

I ran inside and grabbed a dishtowel, my empty shoe box, and a pencil. When I made it back, the cat was definitely interested. Whisker's twitching, long tail lashing, it watched the bird with wide eyes.

The bird hadn't moved, other than its little heart pumping fast. Carefully, I covered it with a dish towel, and then poked holes in the box lid with the pencil. The cat sat, watching me.

"No, I'm not wrapping up your snack. You're going to have to find something else today, buddy."

The cat licked his paw, intentionally ignoring me.

Gently, I scooped up the bird and cradled it in my palm, still wrapped in the towel. I placed the poor little thing in the box and situated the lid over it.

Am I doing this right? I searched up bird rescue on my phone and scanned the advice. From what I saw, so far, so good. They also said the bird needed a safe location and some time to allow the shock to wear off.

"Okay," I whispered. "Let's get you someplace quiet to calm down."

I carried the box into my bedroom and set it in a shaded corner. Once it was settled, I tip-toed out of the room.

Bird in a box, boxes down the road. Boxes at Charlie Booker's place.

I still needed to send the photo of the shoe print to Carlson. As I walked down the stairs, I slid my phone from my pocket. After stabbing a short explanation across the keys with my thumbs, I forwarded it to him.

Then I sank down on the last few boxes of flooring. So many thoughts were spinning in my mind, I didn't think a run would work this time.

A few weeks ago, Kari had tried to get me interested in a little roller ball of essential oils that she carried. It was supposed to help with stress, and seriously, at this point, I could probably use a bucket of it. I knew where to get it, from the Heritage Dispensary, and I'd been meaning to go back to visit anyway. I'd met Mrs. Lavender the owner under less than wonderful conditions, with her gagged and tied up and me running from a gunman. I'd wanted to reintroduce myself and this was a good of time as any. I could also head down to the mall where I purchased my sneakers and see what they had to say about the extra large size. Maybe they had some type of record of a man buying them there.

Wallet and keys located, I climbed back into the car. I rubbed my neck. It was still disconcerting that someone had been in it last night. What could they have done? Put on a tracking device? But why me? My brain scrambled for answers.

I drove down the road and saw Richie working in his front flower bed with a shovel and a wheelbarrow. Seeing him, I slowed down to wave.

He waved back and started toward me, making me stop in the road.

"Hey, what are you doing?" he asked. He took off his cowboy hat and wiped his forehead. "You feeling better?"

"Not so much. Hey, crazy question; you weren't by any chance wearing sneakers last night, were you?"

He arched an eyebrow like I'd just asked him if he'd like a pocket full of raw fish and then he glanced down at his cowboy boots. "That'd be a negative. Can't think of the last time I had on a pair. Maybe for high school gym class."

"That's what I figured. Anyway, I found a shoe print by my

mailbox. I'm pretty sure it's the same type of jogging shoes as I own. Only these are about twice as big."

His eyes widened, making that cute little wrinkle above each eyebrow appear. "You serious? Wow! We need to get a camera out at your place right now! I have a game cam you can borrow for a bit."

"No, I don't need that." I shook my head, not wanting to bother him.

"Seriously, you shouldn't play around with stuff like that; people wandering around your place at night. Come on, I'll go get it. It will give me some peace of mind."

Resigned, I pulled into his driveway and parked. It probably wouldn't hurt.

"You want to go inside and say hello to Ma? She's been asking about you. I'll be right in."

"Okay. See you in a sec." I said.

As I walked up to the porch, I noticed a funnel poking out of the engine of his truck with an upturned bottle of oil in it. The guy was busy.

I glanced up at his home and smiled. The quaint farmhouse spoke of generations of children running up and down the stairs with its smooth spots in the railing where little hands often touched. Baskets filled with petunias hung under the eaves, and the flowers spilled out in a stunning purple waterfall.

The front door was opened to allow fresh air to funnel through the screen. I tapped on the door and then walked inside.

"Hello!" I hollered as I peeked into the living room.

My jaw dropped. Instead of seeing Richie's mom, my gaze fell on Ms. Valentine seated on the couch. She held what looked like a needle and a ball of string in her thin fingers.

Ms. Valentine, Charity's older sister, was a woman who cared for me about as much as a fly on a wedding cake. She looked at me now with lips pursed. As stunned as I was, her expression made me a little concerned about the needle.

"Do you normally just walk into people's homes unannounced?" she said, her voice dripping with its usual sardonic tone.

I snapped my jaw shut from where I'd been gawking like a teenager at a pop star. "I'm sorry! Richie let me in. I'm here to say hi to Truly." My nose wrinkled in a grimace at my limp response. Did I just apologize to her? Why did I let this woman throw me off my game so much?

She sniffed. At that moment Richie's mom popped around the corner. Richie had mentioned Truly was doing better,

CEECEE JAMES

however I was astonished to see the transformation that had taken place.

Clothed in a pale pink blouse and white pants, Truly looked as neat as a pin. Her hair was pulled back in a twist and fastened with a sparkling barrette. Pink toenails appeared in the open toe of white sandals. Bangles chimed on her arms.

"Truly!" I gasped. Ms. Valentine scowled at my response, and I quickly tried to cover. "You look terrific."

"Oh, thank you. It's amazing what new friends can do." Richie's mom held something up. "Look at what Charity has made for me!"

It was a teeny tiny pink doll dress. Delicate lace edged the hem. It was nice to see someone else who appreciated Truly's doll collection as much as she did.

"Charity made that? It's adorable," I gushed.

Truly grinned. "And Gladys is sewing the bonnet. Absolutely breathtaking."

Ms. Valentine's face wavered between the scowl she was still sending my way and pride at her friend's comment. It was then that I identified the pink lacy thing in her hands.

The front door closed and heavy footfalls indicated Richie was finally inside.

He ducked his head around the corner, his hair half falling over his face, his hat clenched in one hand. "Ma, I see your friends are here. Sorry, I must have been in the barn when they arrived." He pushed the hair back and smiled.

"Richie." His mom reached out to him. "Come say hello."

He walked over and greeted Charity. Then, with great gusto, he admired Ms. Valentine's bit of doll clothing she was finishing.

Eventually, he made it over to my side. "I'm going to steal Stella for a bit, if you ladies don't mind."

"Steal her? We couldn't give her away," Ms. Valentine sniffed, clipping a thread.

"You come back soon for a visit, you hear? Maybe come to Bingo with us!" called Truly.

I assured her I would and followed Richie out.

"Come on this way. Have you been back here before? I keep the game camera in the barn."

We walked out into the property. The grass was a beautiful shade of waving green, with a dirt path worn from years of use to the back buildings. Following the grass line was a row of trees, full of leaves and fragrant with flowers.

"Apples?" I asked.

He shook his head. "Nah, these are sweet cherry. We do have some apples growing down in the back."

"By that creek where I hear the frogs chirping from every night?"

He grinned, flashing white teeth. "That'd be the one."

The dirt crunched under our shoes as we headed toward the big red barn. The windows to the hayloft were open like eyes, hay spilling out like eyelashes, as if watching us approach.

"Your mom, she's doing so good," I said.

Just then I slipped on a rock. He reached for my arm to balance me.

"Careful now. You okay?"

I nodded. His hand left me, reluctantly I thought.

He cleared his voice and answered, "She's never been good with change. I think she's still adjusting to her new normal. But Charity and Gladys have been a breath of fresh air for her."

As much as Ms. Valentine and I didn't always get along, I agreed she was proving she really had an amazing side.

He led me into the barn, strong with the scent of engine grease and oil from being converted into a garage. Sitting in one corner was the purple Challenger I'd long coveted.

He saw my glance. "I'll take you for a spin if you want. You just say the word when."

"I'd like that, sometime."

Richie found the camera on a shelf and showed me how to boot it up. There was a simple app to download to my phone. After I downloaded it, he went on his phone and, after pressing a few buttons, he gave me a satisfied smile. "There."

"There what?"

"I just reset the password. Pick whatever you want. Only you have access now to the footage."

"Now you lost your chance to spy on me," I teased.

He laughed. "Not my style. If you want me to come by, you have to go about it the old fashioned way."

"And what's that exactly?"

His eyes twinkled. "I'll send a note. Do you like me? Check the box yes or no."

I laughed. He walked with me back out to the car and waved as I backed out. He was looking pretty cute, all scruffy and sweet as he smiled.

I only had a second to think about it. As I turned sharply back onto the road, I realized what the thieves had taken.

16

I knew what was stolen from my car last night. That dog collar! I had no idea why it could have been important to the thieves, but it was definitely missing. I'd left it on the dashboard, and nearly every corner I'd taken since the day I'd chucked it up there, it had scraped across the vinyl with the turns.

It was gone now.

The thought was so startling, I had to pull over to be sure. I threw on the hazard lights before getting out to check under the passenger seat and floor.

There was no denying it. Someone had taken it.

Dazed, I climbed back in the car and continued toward town.

That meant someone had known I'd had it and had tracked down my home to steal it.

That was the creepiest thought in the world.

What on earth was so special about a broken dog collar that would make someone go through that extreme?

Who could have known I had the collar, anyway? Someone at my work? At the store? I drummed my fingers against the steering wheel, trying to think. I *had* gone to Maribel's house with it on the dash. Had she seen it that day? I thought about the first time I'd seen the footprint by my mailbox—outside of Charlie Booker's duplex.

Okay, the print was from a jogging shoe. The neighbor had mentioned that Maribel, Charlie's sister, jogged. Was it too much of an assumption to think that her boyfriend jogged as well?

Still, it didn't make sense that either one of them would care about the dog collar. Every question kept circling back to, "But why?" Nothing made sense.

Fortunately, I was in Brookfield now, giving me an excuse to take a break from the never-ending questions. I turned off of Main street and onto the road the dispensary was located on, quickly finding a space to park.

I grabbed my purse and climbed out. The wind kicked some leaves past me as I contemplated the two-story brick building. It was built in the flavor of the early historical traditional style. When I'd last been there, the lights were off, leaving the building dark and foreboding. A shiver ran down my spine at the memory. Today, the front door was open with tranquil music spilling out.

I walked up to the door, passing a dandelion growing from a crack in the sidewalk. Its golden shaggy head cast a shadow twice its size down the cement. It was a good reminder to appreciate the beautiful things when I saw them. The whole "take time to smell the roses..." philosophy. Because last time I'd been here had been a sharp reminder that life could turn on a dime.

Next to the dispensary's front door was a watering dish for people who walked by with their dogs. Sweet.

I walked inside the cool building. A buzzer sounded from a hidden motion detector, something new from the last time I was there.

Mrs. Lavender wasn't anywhere in sight. I glanced up at the shelf on the ceiling beam with its joke, "Books for tall people." It made me smile. The scent of patchouli wrapped around me and invited me in further.

I was about to yell a greeting when a woman popped around a

shelf. Around my height and appearing close to my dad's age, the woman's face was pale with nervousness. My heart squeezed. I knew what put that expression there. Still, she was a survivor, as her professional smile proved.

"Oh, hello, there." Her face relaxed at the sight of me. "How can I help you?"

"Mrs. Lavender?" I asked.

Her eyebrows flew up at my words. I realized she must be trying to place my voice. "You sound so familiar," she said slowly.

I smiled. "Well, the first time we met was under rather crazy circumstances. I'm Stella O'Neil."

Her face lit up, and she let out a squeal. "Oh, my gosh! That was you! You saved the day! I'll never forget how you raced past me for the exit! My heart nearly stopped when they shot at you. You *are* okay, right?"

I nodded. "I felt sick with worry that I had to leave you."

She shook her head. "I was worried about you! I could hear them crashing into the shelving, chasing after you." Her hand went to her forehead. "That was a horrific night."

There were no words either of us could add to describe the nightmare. "How are you dealing with it?"

Her finger lifted the pendant at her neck. "Well, I'm wearing Peace right now. I pray a lot. I'm getting through, but it isn't easy."

She was a hero, coming back here to a place where she'd experienced so much terror. She didn't run away from it, instead she'd incorporated it into her story and owned it like a boss.

Warmth at her courage grew inside of me. "You are amazing."

She smiled and shook her head. "Some days I think I'm doing better. Others I'm right back in trauma mode. It's like going around and around the same mountain. Then I realize, I'm making progress every time I have to process it again. How about you? How are you doing?"

I chuckled. "I'm learning there really is no such thing as normal, and I need to be more patient with myself."

"Sounds like you've been down this road before."

Had I? "Not necessarily. I just think I grew up so used to computers and microwaves that I sort of expected the same instant results from myself. So it's been a frustrating lesson to realize that life doesn't necessarily happen like that. But it doesn't mean there's something wrong with how I'm healing."

"I agree." Those worry wrinkles appeared between her

eyebrows again, and she touched her chin. "There's something about you.... Your face. I know it from somewhere else," she finished.

"Oh yeah? I'm new to the area. Relatively, anyway."

"I'm from a town about fifty miles away myself. No, you just look familiar."

Well that was odd. "Maybe I look like my uncle? He owns the Flamingo Realty."

She gave a slight nod as she considered that. I could see her struggling to accept the explanation, and then she shook her head. "No. That's not it. I feel like I know you. Something about your eyes."

Her words hit like a lightning bolt. Eyes. I swallowed hard, scared to proceed, uncertain if I wanted to hear more or not.

A laugh shot out of her. "Of course! You remind me of a friend of mine from high school. Vani Steward. It's been years. Do you know her?"

Chills ran down my back. I'd never known my mother's maiden name. Was it my Vani? It had to be. "I'm not sure. It could be my mom."

"Your mom!" She squinted hard at me as her hand went to her hips before giving a firm nod. "Yep, I can see it. Same eyes. Same dimple in the chin. My goodness, it's been ages. How's she doing?"

"You don't know?"

Her face paled, and she clutched the basket tighter. "Don't tell me she's died?"

I shook my head. "I grew up without her and have only recently been trying to track her down. She...she went to prison."

"Oh, my goodness! Vani?" Her mouth went slack with incredulousness and her wide eyes reminded me of the first desperate moment I'd seen her.

"I guess so," I reluctantly confirmed.

"What on earth? How could that possibly happen? Your mom was nothing like that. A straight A-student. A good kid, really. Lived with her aunt."

"Her aunt?" I leaned closer for more details, feeling like a baby bird being fed for the first time.

"Now that was a mean old biddy. She kept poor Vani under lock and key. I remember once your mom was five minutes late for her curfew. Poor girl was grounded for a month. Missed the Sadie Hawkins dance, she did. And she'd been invited by the quarterback of the football team." Mrs.

Lavender clucked her tongue in remorse. Then her gaze zeroed in on me again. "You *are* going to visit her?"

A thrill twirled in my stomach. Subconsciously, I *had* been planning on something like that, hadn't I?

I nodded. "So one of the reasons I came by today was because I thought I should stock up on something to help," I said, gesturing to the oil in her necklace.

She grabbed at the pendant. "Oh, honey. I'm going to set you up. One thing you need right now is hope. And I have just the oil for it."

TWENTY MINUTES LATER, I was back out on the sidewalk with a new pendant and a bag rattling with a few oils. Mrs. Lavender wouldn't take a payment, insisting it was the least she could do for saving her life. I lifted the filigree heart and took a deep sniff, very thankful for the gift.

But I couldn't dally any longer. I needed to get to the shoe store. Time was ticking away, and I had a few questions to ask.

I fought rush-hour traffic on my way to the mall, and spent another fifteen minutes searching for a parking space in the crowded garage. Every time I thought I found a spot, there was a cracker-box-sized car tucked away in there, tricking me. I gave a victory shout when I finally saw a vacant space and shoe-horned in my car. Why did they make parking so compact? Shaking my head, I locked the door and hurried into the busy mall.

It was packed at this time of the evening, with people gravitating toward the food court for dinner. The scents of orange chicken, pizza and spicy hot wings hit me all at once like a wall of cravings, making my mouth water. I couldn't stop. I wasn't here to eat, but to get some answers.

I knew from my own search for good running shoes that the stores were limited around here who carried the brand with the corkscrew tread. This was the only place I knew of within a fifty mile radius. It was possible that he (I was assuming it was a man by the size of the shoes) had ordered them on line, or even traveled farther. Still this seemed like the easiest explanation.

I knew the shoes couldn't have been Charlie's, because Charlie was not a tall man. And I was positive it wasn't one of the thieves who had been arrested for Charlie's murder. They weren't tall themselves. It had to have been someone else.

That left Maribel's boyfriend.

It was a little frustrating to be dismissed by the police since they hadn't seen the tracks. I got it though. In their eyes, they had their case buttoned up, just the way they liked it. And here I was, trying to blow it all apart. Someone wasn't going to be happy with me.

I just didn't realize how angry they would be.

17

I rode the escalator up to the second floor and then skirted the Playland that was protected by a dozen strollers like they were circling the wagons.

After a quick glance at the time, I sped up as I navigated around the line of people waiting for a frosty orange drink.

Luckily, the shoe store was still open. Even better, the same sales person who'd helped me earlier was working this evening. He'd been a nice guy, who I half suspected had been hitting on me the entire time. Of course, excessive flattery was probably a standard salesman tactic to secure a sale, and I have to admit it might have helped.

"Stella!" he said, his eyes lighting up when he spotted me. "How's the runners?"

A glow rushed through me that he remembered my name. I glanced at his name tag. David. "I love them! Listen, do you have a few minutes? I have a couple questions I wanted to run by you."

He glanced around the empty store. "Sure seems like it. Come on, have a seat." He straightened his tie and waltzed over to a row of chairs. Smiling at me, he pointed to the one next to him. As I sat, he arched an eyebrow and stroked his already swooping hair back.

"So...." His voice dropped several octaves as he moved closer to lean on the arm separating our two chairs. "What can I do for you this evening?"

"I have a question about the shoes. Not mine exactly, the men's version."

The change that came over him couldn't have been more drastic if a lightning bolt came straight down from heaven and parted his hair. He straightened up and fixed the cuff on one of his sleeves, his eyes dropping away from mine. "What size shoe is your boyfriend looking for?"

"Oh, I don't have a boyfriend."

I was fascinated to see him morph back into the shmoozy man he'd been just seconds earlier.

"No boyfriend? I can't believe such a beautiful woman as

yourself isn't already taken." David smiled, showing perfect white teeth as evidence of braces he must have worn during high school. The smile glowed with confidence. This was terrible but it kind of made me want to giggle.

I squashed that completely inappropriate reaction down and allowed myself a smile in response. Just a small one. He was on the hook so he didn't need too much more encouragement.

"So, about these shoes?" He asked as his eyebrows raised in an overly-exaggerated expression of concern and helpfulness.

"Well, it's kind of a weird situation. I'm acting as a bit of a detective."

"Ohh," he nodded approvingly. "Sounds interesting. Let's hear it."

"This is going to sound crazy but my car was broken into the other night. Right in front of my house."

"Whoa! Are you serious!"

"Yes!"

"Did they take anything?"

I hesitated. I couldn't very well tell him they took a dog collar. Instead, I hedged a bit. "A few things that weren't really of value, except to me. Mostly it was beyond creepy."

David nodded. "Do you have your concealed weapon permit?"

"What? No. I don't want to go that route."

"You should think about it. As a woman, you need to protect yourself."

I blinked at him. He was serious. Now wasn't the time to tell him there was no way on God's green earth I was going to be carrying a pistol. Instead, I tried to steer him back to my request.

"I'll consider it. In the mean time, this is where I wanted to see if you could help."

"Ask me anything."

"There were prints in the mud outside my car, left by the guy who broke in."

"You're kidding me?"

"No, and the police missed it. However, I did take a picture."

I found my phone and scrolled through until I found the photo. He took my phone, making a show of being extra careful, and examined it.

"It's the same brand that you bought," he noted with a nod.

"Yes, but these are nearly twice as big. See, look at this one." I scrolled to the picture I'd taken with my foot in the scene.

He whistled. "That's a big shoe."

"Mmhmmm," I agreed.

"I bet that's at least a size fourteen." He rubbed his neck and stared in the corner. I could practically see the hamster wheel in his brain spinning. "We did have a pair. We usually only carry one of that size. And they've been sold."

"Did you sell them?" I leaned forward eagerly.

David shook his head. "No. The runners were gone one day when I came in." He abruptly stood. "You know what? I think I can track them down. Unless the guy paid cash."

He headed behind the counter to the computer.

I jumped up and followed. "Do people normally pay with cash?" I figured it had to be pretty rare.

Instead of reassuring me, he grimaced, his nose wrinkling. "It's a lot more common than you'd think. Some of these gangsters come here for their shoes...." He shrugged like that should explain it.

It was nerve-wracking because he was typing for a while. The longer he typed, the lower his eyebrows went and the more anxious I became. I chewed my thumbnail, feeling a mixture of wanting to run off the nervous energy and needing to throw-up. Was this all going to come to nothing? I clawed at my pendant and gave it a sniff.

"Okay," David said abruptly, scaring me.

"What did you find," I asked, a little breathless.

His hand went to the back of his neck again. "Well, it's not good news. He paid in cash."

"Oh, no." I grabbed the counter, feeling like my world was crashing down. I'd been so hopeful.

"Well, hold on. Everything is not all lost. He left an email."

"An email?"

He glanced in my direction. "Yeah. People sign up so they can get coupon breaks and stuff." He reached in a drawer for paper and a pen. Carefully, he scribbled. Chicken scratch, but I was charmed to see he was left handed. He tossed the pen back in the drawer and passed the paper over.

My jaw dropped when I read it. Deaddriftnymph@nw.com

Nymph.

Like the name on the dog tags I'd found. The ones on the collar that had been stolen from my car.

David noticed my reaction. "Hey, you okay? Does this mean something to you?"

Still wrapped in shock, I nodded. I think he was disappointed when I walked toward the door. I felt like I was floating. "Thanks for your help, David."

"Uh, yeah. Is there anything else I can do?"

My head was shaking no, but I answered, "I'll let you know. Thanks again."

"All right, well..."

I lifted my hand numbly and waved goodbye. He deserved a better response, but honestly, I could barely think to form a sentence. I was so overwhelmed. I needed to get by myself so I could process.

Traffic wasn't as bad on my drive home. My list of chores was growing. I needed to message Carlson, and I needed to get that camera working. Who was this guy? Was his name really DeadDrift?

I had the creepy-crawlies when I pulled into my driveway. I shut the car door, staring for more footprints. Not seeing any, I ran up the porch stairs and unlocked the door.

My plan to message Carlson was derailed by a few chirps. It sounded like my little bird friend had recovered.

I tip-toed into my bedroom where little scrabbles of bird claws welcomed me. I didn't chance checking on the bird's well-being in the house. With my luck, he'd escape and then where would I be? I'll tell you where. I'd be up all night trying to cajole a bird down from the rafters with bread crumbs.

I carefully carried the box out into the lawn and set it down in the new soft grass. Slowly, I lifted the lid. Black beady eyes met mine as the bird tipped his head.

"Hi, buddy," I whispered.

The bird hopped a few steps.

"How are you feeling?"

He looked around for a moment and then, with a flutter of his wings, flew up into my face.

"Ohh!" I cried, falling back startled.

He landed on my shoulder and I froze, unsure of what to do. He was so light, I never would have felt him if not for his tiny hops.

After a second, I relaxed. In fact, I was grinning from ear to ear as I realized what an incredibly gift this was. The bird bounced a bit to the edge of my shoulder. After another quick look around, and with a windy flutter of his wings, he was off.

A pang of loss shivered through my happiness. I was glad that he was okay. "Bye, friend."

I spotted him up in a tree, a dark silhouette in the dusky light. With a final wave, I walked back inside. It was time to set up the camera by my front door, as well as send Carlson a text message of everything new that I'd learned today. Surely, now he'd believe me that they had the wrong guys. Maybe he'd finally investigate Maribel and her boyfriend a little more. My gut was telling me something was wrong at that place, and I knew more than anything, I better trust that hunch.

18

---

*C*arlson wasn't happy that I had neglected to tell him about the dog collar I'd found at the duplex on the day of Charlie Booker's murder. Seriously, I don't blame him. At the time, it had crossed my mind that maybe the person had seen the murderer and that's why the dog escaped. But, with everything that had happened since, I'd forgotten all about it.

I will say, he did try to eat some humble pie about his attempt to convince me that it had been a car backfire that I'd heard the other night. And he said he believed it gave more weight to the intent of the threatening letter I'd received. He wouldn't give me any more details other than to say they were searching through camera footage from several places.

"Did you ever find out anything more about the boxes I found under the bridge?"

"Listen, Hollywood. You're on a need to know basis, and right now, you don't need to know."

I ignored him and carried on. "Because I was thinking about that one neighbor with all the dogs that I'd met. He said he'd had a bunch of people traipsing through the back half of his property. There's a river back there."

Carlson grunted.

"I wondered if maybe that's where the boxes got dumped off."

"And why would they be dumped there?" he asked.

"Well, the day we were showing the house, I noticed a ton of boxes in one of the rooms at Charlie Booker's house."

"Because he was moving."

Why did everyone always say that? "Maybe. Or maybe he was that big ring leader the cops are looking for in the box truck thefts."

There was a heavy exhale. "Tell me the truth. Do you have another lead on the force?" he finally asked.

"What do you mean?"

"A snitch? An *in*?"

"Just you. Why?" I asked.

"I'll just tell you we're working on it."

"Oh, well, yay!" I grinned. "I guess I'm on the right track."

"Wrong," he said. "You're on no track. Your job is to sell houses and stay safe."

"Got it," I answered meekly. His voice was too grouchy to argue with. Besides, I knew I hadn't done anything wrong. I wasn't poking my nose where it didn't belong. I just happened to have a knack for finding things.

Sort of like Oscar and his FBI career. Maybe it was in the blood after all.

Carlson and I hung up, leaving me to mull over family bloodlines. My meeting with Mrs. Lavender had been next level stuff. I'd actually reminded her of my mom. Things were coming so fast, and I was learning new things about my mom that I hadn't known my entire life but at the same time the questions kept piling up.

Which pushed me into a new decision. I was going to the prison to visit my mother, wasn't I? After all, who else could answer all the questions I had?

Seeing Mrs. Lavender pushed the urgency to make the visit happen. I couldn't forget the first time I'd met the business woman, and it brought home how short life truly was. What if something happened to my mom? To me? I needed to do this before I lost my chance.

I also needed to do it before I lost my guts. That wasn't a nice thing to say, but I knew myself well enough that if I took too much time to think about it, I would talk myself out of it. Even moving to Pennsylvania—I did it after two-week's of serious consideration. I was a jumper, I guess.

And it was time to take another leap of faith.

———

Luckily, or very unluckily, depending how you viewed it, I didn't have any new house showings the next morning, so my day was completely empty. Unfortunately, so was my wallet. Still, showered, dressed, snacks packed and oil necklace drenched, I was keeping myself positive as I climbed into the car for a journey of a lifetime—a visit to the state prison.

I won't lie, I gave a little shiver every time I sat behind the wheel, thinking about some stranger snooping through my car. Especially if it was the murderer.

I'd gotten a text earlier with Carlson asking me to bring in my car so they could dust for fingerprints. He thought it was highly unlikely that they'd find any, considering how I'd been in and out of the vehicle. Still, he said it was worth a shot. I'd asked if we could wait until the afternoon, and he seemed to be okay with it.

The prison was over an hour away. An hour turned out to be the longest time in existence when you knew that what lay at the end of it was about to change your entire world forever.

More anxiety flushes. I reached into my purse and grabbed a package of mints. Sometimes, something sweet helped to stave off the nerves for a bit.

Ten minutes later, I'd crunched through the whole pack and the worry was as strong as ever.

Okay then, You're just going to have to do this regardless of how you feel. Fake it, Stella. Pretend you're cool and in control.

The directions led me off the highway and up a narrow road into the hills. *This is it. I'm visiting a prison.* I tried to catch any sort of glimpse of the building through the trees. Eventually, the entrance into the prison parking lot could be seen.

It was intimidating. The guard tower had at least three guards glaring down at me as I drove up. It was like they just knew I was doing something wrong. I felt guilty for no reason. One of the guards asked who I was there to see and then asked for my ID. I showed him, my license nearly slipping from my shaking fingers.

Someone unseen buzzed me in. Unfortunately, that was only the first step. I found a numbered parking spot and moved my car in, and then walked to the second gate. From there I was hustled through metal detectors, beepers, and pat downs. I had to get my picture taken, my purse examined, and go through more detectors.

Each part of the process led me closer to my goal. My heart pounded but I walked with determined steps, my footfalls against the linoleum stating, "Going to see mom, going to see mom." It was surreal.

There were other people on this weird journey down the long prison hallway with me: older women walking with children, husbands, and more relatives. I eyed a little girl sucking her thumb, perched on the hip of her grandma like a little koala bear. Would that young one know her mom still?

"Next!" yelled a security guard at the last station I needed to get through. My legs felt like noodles as I walked over to the desk. There was a woman behind the glass, her lips held in a stern frown, hair cut in a short bob. I passed her my ID.

She stared at for a minute, her lip moving like she was chewing a piece of tough meat. Then she clicked on her keyboard. Her fingers moved in slow motion, my pulse keeping beat with every key push.

She chewed some more, then stared at me. "I'm sorry, you're not cleared for visitation."

"What?" I said, breathless.

"We don't have details here. You'll need to contact her attorney."

And, just like that, the whole bottom fell out of my world. After all these years of lies, deceit. To be denied my mom, AGAIN. I wanted to smash the glass window, rip the papers, thrown a chair.

The security officer must have caught the fury in my eye. "Calm down," she warned.

Wrong words. My hands started to shake as horrible violent thoughts flashed through my head. I wanted to punch someone. Punch her!

"This isn't my fault. You can contact her lawyer and find out what's going on. This decision isn't up to me." Her eyes softened. "It seems to be what she wants."

She wanted to be left alone? My mom, who now essentially abandoned me for a second time? I was so angry, I couldn't respond. I swiped up my license and stormed out, not caring if people were in the way. Luckily, there weren't. I wasn't in my right mind to hold anything back. The storm raged inside, breaking through the wall I'd so carefully tended to all those years.

I slammed the exterior doors open and strode outside. Bright sunshine made me wince, but I couldn't be bothered to dig through my purse for the sunglasses. Let my eyes water. I didn't care. Bring it on.

Every thought after that was just as ridiculous. I wanted to kick the car fender and hoped it would leave a dent. I wanted to punch the light pole, relishing the idea of the pain it would make me feel.

I did none of these things. Instead, I unlocked the door and climbed into an already hot car. Sinking my head against my hands that desperately clutched the steering wheel like it was a life ring, my soul let loose. I couldn't hold back the tears.

Why? Why? Why? Was there some mistake? After the letter I'd sent, she had to be prepared that I was coming. Why would she do this to me? Why would she deny me again?

She didn't want to meet me.

She didn't want me at all.

I smacked the steering wheel, the pain immediately satisfying and also proving that I really didn't want to take hitting things too much further. I leaned my head back against the seat, tears falling, and stared out at the simmering parking lot.

Ripples of heat rose from the cracked pavement. How many tears had this place seen?

Well, they wouldn't see anymore of mine. I wiped my face on my arm. If she didn't want to see me, fine. I didn't want to see her either.

I jammed the key into the ignition and started the car. Staring over the back of my seat, I gave it more gas than I should have, as the vehicle jerked out of the stall. I threw the gearshift into drive and stomped on the gas again, zooming past the guard tower, shaking the dust off my feet as I went.

19

The drive home gave me more time to think. Maybe the word "think" was too specific. More like it gave me time to calm down. Still, I wasn't feeling very companionable, so I sent a voice text to Carlson to ask if we could reschedule the fingerprinting. I wasn't too hopeful, but I had to ask.

Instead of texting back, he called. "What's wrong, Hollywood?"

My eyebrows lifted. How could he possibly have known there was something wrong through a simple text? "I just don't feel well, and was hoping I could head straight home."

A couple seconds of silence passed as he processed. "Not

feeling well, huh? Go on home and I'll get the crew out there to dust it at your house."

I thanked him, though the word "crew" gave me the heebie-jeebies. My mood was "operation hide from all people." Still, I wanted to catch the person who broke into my car and who was possibly the murderer of Charlie Booker, so we set a time for later in the afternoon.

After visiting the drive-through of my favorite restaurant—the brown bag crinkling with promises of greasy, carb-ladened kaka—I drove home. Upon getting out, a bird trilled from the pine tree. I wondered if it was my little friend I'd rescued. I thought about tearing a chunk of the bun into crumbs, but I couldn't do that to the little guy. I went inside for a bag of unsalted sunflower seeds that I'd been using for pancakes and sprinkled them outside instead. Then I sat on my last two boxes of flooring and ate my food, staring morosely at the unfinished project.

To say that I was in the depths of despair was putting it lightly. I was questioning everything. My internal gut—why did I think my mother would ever want to see me? My judgment of others—I would have never suspected the three men in my life would have been lying to me all this time. Even my own existence. I was going down the toilet bowl of "who cares about me?" as I slurped my soda, making an obnoxious noise at the bottom that echoed my own drowning thoughts.

My own pity trip was making me sick. *Enough of this.* I stood up, and immediately unbuttoned my pants, then headed to the kitchen with the garbage.

As I turned, my toe literally caught the edge of one of the last boxes of laminate. It made me mad, but it also proved I needed to get the job done. It was just another weight hanging around my neck right now.

I chugged back the last bits of French fries from their container like it was a shot of whiskey and then grabbed my utility knife. The blade cut through the shrink-wrapped plastic with a satisfying zip. Peeling it back, I revealed what I hoped was one of the last stacks of flooring I needed. The floor was finished to the far corner where I'd run out of steam the other night. I pulled out my tape measure and measured the space then drew the length on the back of the board, making sure the click part was on the correct side. Too many times I'd cut the right length only to discover the locking mechanism was on the wrong side when I flipped it back over. After I did this to a few pieces, I carried my pile out to the garage where I kept the chop saw.

I opened the garage door to let in some light. The little bird chirped at me some more, and I noticed most of the seeds were gone. It didn't quite bring a smile to my face, but my chest lightened.

My chop saw sat in the middle of the floor, surrounded by sawdust and leftover boards. With one zip, it made quick work of cutting. I finished the rest of the pile and then carried the boards back to the corner with anticipation building that I was almost done.

As I kneeled to tap in the next piece, I noticed a small hole in the baseboard. I bent to look at it, curious, even going so far as to stick my finger in it until the vision of a mouse on the other side made me jerk back.

Now, I had a gerbil as a kid. My white hot memories of him were of sharp nips to my fingertips. Gerry had definitely been for looking at, not for touching.

I stared at the hole now. It was probably nothing except another sign that several things around here still needed a loving touch. However, that was getting patched up. STAT.

I reached for the phone and did a quick search on how to repair rodent holes. The top suggestion was to stuff the hole with a metal cleaning pad. Well, just my luck, I had a box of them in the garage left over from the previous tenant. I headed back out there, musing more about gerbils. The last time I'd been to a pet store, I'd only seen hamsters, mice, rabbits and guinea pigs. Was there some sort of gerbil shortage I didn't know about? I needed to ask Kari about it. She had young kids, she had to be up on kid pets.

Speaking of Kari, I wonder how she was feeling? She sure had been sick the last I'd seen her.

Something about the physical act of working was helping my mood, even if I couldn't put my finger on exactly what it was. I smiled a bit as I passed the chop saw, happy that I was almost done.

I stopped dead in my tracks. What was that?

Red droplets sprinkled the ground by the saw.

Had I cut myself? Horrified, I checked my hands, my legs.

Nothing.

What on earth had happened? I walked around the saw slowly, trying to discern anything out of place. There was the stack of debris from where I'd toss the leftover pieces. My safety glasses. A pencil. Sawdust.

I glanced through the open garage door. No one was nearby.

That I could see.

I hurried to the side of the metal door frame and peered out.

Birds chirped in the distance. The wind softly blew the leaves of the crab apple tree in the front yard. For a moment, I feared maybe the neighbor's cat had somehow gotten hurt in the garage. That fear evaporated when I saw my car.

Written on the windshield, in bright red, were the words "You can't save your mom."

I reeled back, bumping into the corner of a shelf. Someone had been here. Right now.

My gaze darted about. They couldn't have left that long ago. Had I heard a car? I stared out at the road, hoping to see something. No car, although there was what looked suspiciously like a cloud of dust in the air.

I ran my fingers through my hair and crouched to the ground. I couldn't take this anymore. I really couldn't. A mental collapse curved around the edges of each breath threatening to overtake me. I covered my mouth and tried to prevent hyperventilation.

I glanced up, taking slow breaths. It was then I saw the bloom of dust on the road grow bigger. My eyes widened. They were coming back! I had to get out of here!

I was about to dash inside the house when I realized it was a police car. Carlson.

I ran down the driveway to meet him. His eyes were wide with concern as he stared through the windshield while parking the car. Honestly, I was a hot mess. It was then I remembered to button my pants.

"I knew something was wrong," he said, slamming the door.

I did something completely uncharacteristic. I ran toward him, needing a human touch. Needing a hug.

He knew it immediately and drew me in. It wasn't the greatest hug, what with his chest stiff with a bullet-proof vest and odd metal things jabbing at me. Still, it was a comfort.

"What's going on, Stella?" he asked, giving me one more quick pat on the back before gently pushing me away so he could study my face.

There was too much. I couldn't get it all out. Gulping and trying to catch my breath, I pointed to the windshield. Several of the letters dripped.

"There's blood on my saw as well," I whispered.

He walked over and examined it. I nearly fainted when he dipped his finger in the liquid and rubbed it against his thumb. "No, it's not blood. It's not coagulating."

That word made my world spin. Oh, look at the pretty stars...

He must have noticed because the next thing I knew, he was easing me down to the ground. "You're okay, Stella. Breathe. Draw on your strength. It's just paint."

I appreciated his tough love. I nodded and took a few deep breaths. When he was satisfied I was okay, he wandered over to my garage.

"They were just here, then," he noted.

I nodded. "So was I. Actually, I'd just finished cutting a few floorboards. For a second, I thought I'd cut myself."

"Did you noticed if you'd been followed home?"

"No." But would I have even noticed? I was so up in my head on the drive back.

"What's the story about your mom?" he asked, referring to the threat.

I swallowed hard. Here it was... I was about to reveal the big kahuna. "She's in prison. I only found her recently. In fact, I went to see her today."

He glanced at me sharply but didn't respond.

"She wouldn't see me," I whispered.

A sigh escaped him like a balloon losing all of its air. "I can see why you are so upset."

I nodded.

"Who knew you were going?"

"No one."

"Who else knows about your mom?"

That was a rational question. One I should have thought of when I received the first letter. But I'd thought it was a mistake, or maybe a weird prank. Obviously, it wasn't. I listed everyone who knew about my mom. "My family, Kari. Richie and you."

"Richie knows?"

I nodded. He sighed again. "Well, the forensic team should be here any minute. We'll have this all checked out. In the meantime, maybe you should stay in a hotel tonight."

I didn't answer as another thought came to me.

There was one other person who knew about my mom.

*M*aribel. The woman who had my notebook. And she just so happened to be my main suspect for Charlie Booker's murder.

I remembered Richie's animal camera where I'd set it on a flower pot by the front door. I jumped up and strode into the house, leaving Carlson to gape after me. What was that app again? I scrolled through my phone's menu until I found it, and then looked for the text I'd sent myself with the password.

My hands were shaking as I typed it in. A moment later, the black screen showed the scene outside. I watched Carlson shake his head as he stared at my house. Then he got out his camera and began taking pictures of the words on my car. A moment later, another car pulled in with the forensic team.

What had happened earlier? Was there a rewind button on this thing? I pushed an unfamiliar symbol, hoping for a drop-down menu. Instead, what I got was "Delete?"

No! No! I stabbed at the menu, trying to make the question disappear. It was of no use. I didn't want to mess this up. I laced up my running shoes, tied my hair back in a ponytail, and returned outside.

"You going somewhere?" Carlson asked, one eyebrow lifted. The sun reflected blindingly off the car's windshield where another officer was inside. Carlson took off his hat and swiped at the sweat on his bald dome.

"I'll be right back," I reassured him.

"Before you go, I really want you to tell me that you're staying someplace else for tonight. Just until we figure this out. I mean, it's twice now that they've come to your house. I just don't think it's a good..."

"Let's talk about this later," I said and started jogging. This was more than I could contemplate.

On my way down the driveway, I kept my eyes out for more shoe prints. The ground was as dry as a bone with nothing that my untrained eye could detect.

I had jogged about half-way to Richie's house when I realized he might not even be home. I should have texted first instead of showing up all sweaty and dirty like I'd just squirmed out from the house's crawl-space. There was nothing for it now. I needed his help, and I was just going to have to hope he was home to give it.

I jogged down the driveway, briefly congratulating myself on how my stamina had improved and ran up the stairs to the front porch.

"Oh, my!" Truly gasped in surprise from where she'd been tucked behind a large display of flowers with her watering can.

I squealed as I swung around. I'd scared her as much as she'd scared me.

"Hi, Truly." I smiled. "Is Richie home?"

"No, honey. I'm sorry, he's not."

I pressed my lips together, trying to hide my disappointment.

"Are you all right?" she asked, her voice heavy with concern.

Wow. I must really look like a wreck. "I'm fine. I just had some questions about how to work that animal camera of his."

"Oh? Has he gotten you out hunting with him, then?"

I shook my head, smiling slightly. Like *that* would ever happen.

"Okay, then. Just be careful of the Big Oogle."

"The what?" My eyebrows raised almost as high as my voice. What was this now?

She giggled. "That's what my brothers and I used to call it. The Big Oogle. Down by the river there are several culvert pipes. When the wind blows down them, it makes a loud ooogly noise like a giant animal coming to eat you up!" Here she curled her fingers and growled.

I jumped. Where had I heard that noise before?

Out behind Charlie Booker's house, that's where.

I thanked Truly and then headed back to my house. Carlson was inside my car by the time I returned. The other cop car had left.

Standing in the driveway, my chest heaving as I tried to catch my breath, I sent Richie a text asking him how to rewind the footage on the animal cam. After sending it, I walked over and tapped on the car window.

Carlson's head popped up, his gaze slightly pop-eyed.

"Oh, I'm sorry. I didn't mean to scare you."

"I just don't get it," Carlson whispered under his breath as he eased his girth from my little car.

"Get what?" I asked. When he sounded worried, it made me worried.

His eyes were no less concerned when he turned toward me. "We have the group in custody. I can't imagine why they're coming after you at all."

"Maybe because you have the wrong people?" It came out just as grumpy as I felt. It had been a long horrible day, and I wasn't about to pull any punches. The way I was feeling right now, I could punch something. Maybe I *should* stop at the gym.

Air hissed between his clenched teeth. I didn't think he was too happy about the situation either. "You staying at a friend's then?" he pressed.

"Probably not." It came out a little more bluntly than I intended.

"What? I need you to stay—"

"I'll stay at a hotel," I interrupted. I actually thought it was a good idea, and not just for safety reasons. Honestly, I needed a neutral space to have an internal "talking moment." I cringed as I realized I'd used Oscar's words for 'deep thinking'.

He nodded. "Okay, good. I'm almost done here."

I went inside and packed my stuff for an overnight stay. This weird, lonely feeling draped over me like a heavy shawl as I came down the stairs. It was strange to be leaving. It felt too much like running away. But there it was. Better safe than sorry.

I had three boards left on my floor. By heavens, before I left today, I was going to have this floor done. I dropped the duffle bag by the door and went back to the boards. First, I stuffed the hole with the steel wool, and then I laid the last few pieces. As I tapped the last one in, tears sprung into my eyes. Prideful ones. I did it. I laid this entire floor that would be used in the future for years by people, maybe families, after my time was over in this house. I kissed my fingertips and rubbed them against the last board, thankful to leave my mark.

There was a tap on the front door. Carlson stood on the other side uneasily.

"Okay. All done here. I'll let you know what we've found. I..err...I sprayed off your windshield." He didn't ask that I come down to the station to be fingerprinted. He knew I already had.

"Thanks, Carlson," I said.

"Stay safe." He gave me a bob of his head and a serious stare down.

I assured him I would. After he drove away, I checked that all my doors in the house were locked and left for a hotel downtown. I checked myself in and then dropped the duffle on the bed. I was starving.

There was an attached restaurant, but my eye was on the 24-hour convenience store across the street. Honestly, some days just called for a chili dog, a snowball, and a slushy. I threw a bag of corn nuts on the counter at the last moment, paid the bored attendant who barely slid his attention away from the overhead TV to take my money, and then carried my loot up to my room.

Then, door locked, shoes off, blankets pulled back, I climbed into the bed and snapped on the TV. After a rotation through the channels which never seemed to line up in an order I recognized, I finally settled on a murder mystery. I leaned back against the stack of pillows and chowed on the hot dog. Taking a few slurps of the slushy, I grabbed my purple pad and a pen.

The first page still had my mother's name written all over it. No, I wasn't going to think about her anymore. I needed a break from that. Instead, I was going to find out who was trying to scare me, because heck if I was going to take it lying down.

My cell phone blinked with a notification for a voice mail. It turned out to be from Richie, answering my texted question with the directions on how to work the animal camera's rewind function. He ended with a sweet goodbye. "You call me if you need anything, okay? I'll even bring you a piece of homemade pie. I promise I didn't make it."

Richie's funny voice mail brought another layer of confusion. He was cute. I liked his mom. At the same time, was it fair to him to pursue something deeper than friendship with him? He hadn't come straight out and said anything, but a girl could tell.

His relationship with his mom made me smile. This guy relocated his busy shop to those cramped barn quarters, just so he could keep an eye on her after his dad died. That was pretty amazing. Any girl would be lucky to have him.

Was I that girl? I felt like a hot mess, and it was definitely unfair to tangle anyone else into my drama.

I thought of Carlson. After everything he'd been through, he deserved someone stable and normal, too.

I loaded the camera app on my phone. There was a tense moment when I worried something was wrong, then the video sprang right into a black box.

It was dark out. I'd forgotten to leave the porch light on when I left. A critter walked up the stairs. As it hopped onto my porch swing, I recognized the neighbor's cat.

Other than that, nothing was going on. Using Richie's

directions, I rewound it to earlier in the day. There was Carlson walking around my car with his forensic team. He squatted down to examine something in the dirt—maybe a footprint I'd missed?

I rewound even more and saw myself approaching the car and then freezing as I read the message. Almost there...just a little bit further. My heart thumped as I pressed the rewound button again.

Nearly there...

It happened so fast, I almost missed it. A figure in a hoodie ran up to my car and wrote on the windshield with a paintbrush dipped in a container. He stared at my house with sunglasses shielding his eyes, before darting out of sight. I presumed that was when he dripped the paint on my saw. The next scene showed the person running down the driveway.

I watched it again, trying to see it with detective eyes, instead of from an offended victim point of view. The first thing I noticed was a cloud of dust at the beginning of the scene. This seemed to indicate he or she arrived by a car that was beyond the lens of the camera.

As the person ran up to the car, I zoomed in on the shoes. A smile crossed my face when I recognized the huge running sneakers. Okay, same person then.

I zoomed out and watched it again. The person had to deeply bend at the waist to reach the windshield. I needed to do a test to see how my body was positioned when I did it, but I felt like this further proved he was very tall.

I sighed in disappointment. Maribel was not a very tall person. Could it be her boyfriend?

But what about that glimmer on his finger on the hand that holding the can? Was it a wedding ring? I nodded to myself. It was on the right finger. And below that the person wore a watch, one of those health tracker kinds.

It reminded me of a similar flash I'd seen in my uncle's security camera at the Flamingo Realty. I'd like to see that film again. Did I still have the password for it?

I searched for the realty's security site and then log in. I did have the password, but the footage didn't go back past twenty-four hours. I was about to get really bummed out when I remembered I'd taken a picture of the footage with my phone. I pulled it up.

This shot was as grainy as I remembered when trying to study the video. There was a figure's hand as he slid something under my windshield wiper. I zoomed in. There was the same watch.

I leaned back against the pillows and opened the corn nuts. I tossed a few in my mouth, satisfied by the crunch. Now I just needed to find the person who had those shoes and a watch. The same person who also had a dog they may have lost at the scene of the crime.

I crunched some more. *Listen up, buddy. You think you're coming for me, but you don't realize I'm really coming after you.*

21

The next morning, ringing ripped through my dream. I woke slowly, in that soft gray light that makes you think you're floating, while the shrieking phone insisted that reality was about to hit and hit hard. I rolled over and blearily looked around. Something was hard on my face. I reached up and picked off a corn nut, then stared at it curiously.

Where am I and what's happening?

The phone rang again, settling down from the screaming tones from my dream. I lunged for it and read the name. Mrs. Crawford, my landlord.

I answered, thinking I could fool her that I'd been awake for a long time. "Hello?" Unfortunately, my froggy voice gave me away.

"Oh, dear, I'm sorry. Did I wake you?"

The lie rolled off my tongue like butter melting off a hot corn cob. "No, I was just...sitting here."

"Wonderful. And how are you?"

I squinted in the sunlight and pushed myself up in the bed. Where the heck was I, again? Memories flashed back. Hotel room. Bloody letters. "I'm good."

"Terrific. And how is the flooring going?"

Flooring? Oh, yeah. "Uh, I just finished yesterday. It went surprisingly well, minus a few oopsies." I cringed as I said that. Why on earth would I share that with her?

"Oopsies, huh?" She laughed. "That sounds about right. I don't think you can get a project done without a handful of those."

"Do you want to stop by to see it?" I flushed, both from pride in how amazing it worked, and fear that she'd hate it.

"Why, I'd love to. I can swing out later this morning. Will that work for you?"

"Absolutely," I said, springing up from the bed. "In about two hours?"

"Sounds great! See you then."

I checked out of the hotel and ran to my car like a grizzly bear was hot on my heels. All I could think about was how the house might look. When had I last cleaned the bathrooms? Were there dishes in the sink?

My speedster tendencies skidded to a proper pace at the sight of the nose of a police car poking out from behind the cement median. No tickets for me today, thank you. But, once on my road, the race car driver in me broke loose and I barreled down the road in a cloud of dust.

I parked and hurtled up the porch stairs and into the house. As I ran through to the kitchen, every mess jumped out at me.

I spent the next hour cleaning like a Tasmanian devil. The garage needed to be tidied as well. I blanched at the thought of seeing the fake blood so I left that mess for another time and focused on the interior instead.

I made a pitcher of ice tea and cleared out my sink. Finally, after a sweep of the new floor and the fastest shower in history, I sat at the kitchen table with damp hair and my first cup of coffee.

A bird hopped on the railing outside. I wasn't sure if it was my little buddy, but I grabbed some sunflower seeds anyway and tiptoed out on the back porch. "Here you go, handsome," I said as I sprinkled them.

Moments later, the front doorbell rang. I hurried back inside and down the hall. Checking through the window showed Mrs. Crawford's old Cadillac in the driveway. I opened the door to see her standing gracefully in a floral airy shirt and white pants, with a small basket in her hand.

She smiled gently. "Stella! Don't you look wonderful!"

"Thank you! You look amazing as always!"

She waved her hand to dismiss the compliment. "Please. By the way, I found this on your doorstep."

She held out an envelope.

The blood froze in my veins like shards of ice hurtled through them. No. Not again. Had he followed me from the hotel? I involuntarily took a step back like she was holding the tail of a snake. "Where did you find this?"

"Sitting on your mat." She tipped her head at me curiously. "I think I must be missing a story here."

I took it from her with trembling hands. Sweat broke out on my hairline. Slowly, I flipped the envelope over, my stomach mimicking the motion in fear of what I'd see.

Ashmount Penitentiary

A huge breath gusted out of me as I reeled back in relief, grabbing on to the door stop. I vaguely wondered why the mailman would put it on my doormat, but fiery curiosity consumed me. This was from the prison my mother was in.

"Can I come in?" Mrs. Crawford asked.

Where the heck were my manners? "Of course!" I stumbled away from the doorway. "Please come in!"

She glided in, her linen pants making hardly a whisper. "Well, my goodness," she remarked, her eyes lighting up at the finished entryway. "This is so beautiful! You did this?"

"Yep," I answered, staring at the envelope. I cleared my throat and tried to pull myself back into the present. "Let me show you the rest of it."

Mrs. Crawford shook her head. "Stella, it's of no use. You're as flighty as a hummingbird by a feeder. What's going on?"

I pressed my lips together before giving in. Hand still trembling, I lifted the envelope. "It's my mother." A half second later I realized she didn't know what I meant. However, you'd never know it from her calm gaze as she waited for me to continue. "Please, will you come sit down?"

"Certainly." She lifted the basket. "I brought my lemon tea cookies. Perhaps I could go make some tea?"

Geez, the letter had really thrown me for a loop. I'd forgotten the pitcher of iced tea I'd prepared for her visit. "I have some already made. Please, go sit in the living room. I'll be right there." I was so shaken, I pointed in the direction of the living room. The fact that this had once been her house was not registering.

She was ever gracious. "In here?" she nodded. "My, you've done such a lovely job of it." She walked past me in a scented cloud of lavender.

I galloped into the kitchen, my socks sliding on the laminate as I took the corner. Quickly, I assembled ice-filled glasses on a tray (I knew how proper Mrs. Crawford was) and filled them with tea. I selected a slender vase to set in the center and then crept out to the back porch to grab a fistful of forget-me-knots growing by the steps. Then, snagging my letter and trying not to spill the drinks, I headed back to where she waited.

"Oh, what a treat!" Her eyes lit up at the sight. She always made me feel like I was an amazing hostess. I set the tray down on the coffee table where she'd already laid out a tin lined with a linen napkin and layered with sugar-dusted lemon cookies.

She took a glass and carefully brought it to her lips for a small sip. "Mmm," she murmured. "Just the way I like it. Please, help yourself to a cookie. Maybe you should fortify yourself before we jump into the gossip. I'm in no rush at all."

It was kind of her but I couldn't eat. My tongue felt as dry as carpet as I took out the letter. "My mom," I squeaked. "I've been looking for her. She's been the family secret all these years."

Mrs. Crawford gently nodded, the kind expression of patience and caring softening her eyes.

"I found her at Ashmount Penitentiary." Here I flipped the envelope over so she could see the address.

"Let me just get my readers on," She pulled up a jeweled necklace around her neck and put on a pair of red-framed glasses. Her lips pursed, she scanned the return address before sliding the glasses off with a quick nod. "My goodness. You must be on pins and needles. Perhaps it would be better if I go? I don't want to intrude on such a special moment."

I hardly knew if I wanted to be alone or not up until then, when the thought of her leaving suddenly made me panic. What if my mother said she never wanted to hear from me again? After the rejection at the prison, I needed all the support I could get for what I was about to read.

"Please stay," I blurted.

"Stella, it would be my honor," said Mrs. Crawford. Her support nearly made me cry. "So this is the first you've heard from her then. Since you were a child?"

The lump grew in my throat, and I blinked back tears, giving her a quick nod. "I was about five."

"Honey," Mrs. Crawford whispered.

I heaved in a few breaths, trying to calm down, trying to find that steel will of strength to deal with whatever she might have said. Even worse, what if this was the prison informing me that something had happened to her? Could she have possibly died?

That thought spurred me on, and I tore open the letter.

The first few words caused tears to pour down my face.

"Stella, my little star. It's with great gratitude and grief that I send you this letter. Gratitude that my daughter, a playful, beautiful, bold warrior, has contacted me. Your grandfather has kept me updated about you through the years. Hearing about your success has been my heart and soul during times where I've wondered why I am still alive. Receiving your letter has made the long wait so worth the fight.

There is so much I want to talk to you about, and I pray we will have many more opportunities. However, before we can go forward, I have to visit the past.

My darling daughter, the grief comes from my biggest regret that I did something so selfish as to leave you. Please forgive me. You have ultimately paid the price through the loss of what you should have had, what you deserved to have. A mother, to guide, teach, and encourage you, to be your biggest cheerleader and your greatest support. I am so sorry you were robbed of that. I only hope you can someday forgive me."

My voice cut out at this point and I couldn't continue. Tears dripped down my face.

"I'm sorry," I whispered to Mrs. Crawford.

"Nonsense. This is how strong women grieve. We cry even as we move forward. You've made me very proud with your courage."

"She says she doesn't want to talk more unless we talk about the past."

"Your mother is wise. My grandmother used to tell me you don't put new wine in old skins. Your mom knows the only way to move forward is to start new, and starting new means putting the past to bed. I'm glad she's owning her mistakes and asking for forgiveness."

I wiped my face and took a sip of tea. It was happening. I'd come to Pennsylvania to pull my family back together. Well, I never thought a mother was in that equation, yet ultimately, my goal was happening.

"Thank you, Mrs. Crawford."

She softly laughed. "Oh, honey. Every family tree has some

crazy twists and turns. One of these days, I'll tell you about mine. Now have a cookie. Don't make me devour them all myself."

I smiled. "These are good. I rarely eat homemade cookies."

"What? You don't like to bake?"

I shook my head. "They rarely make it past the cookie dough stage."

She smiled and lifted a cookie as if to salute me. "Me as well. I knew from the moment I met you that we were kindred spirits, my friend."

22

I hummed as I cleared the dishes after Mrs. Crawford left. The visit was so good for my soul. And then the letter! Wow!

I packed the letter in my special rose-carved box and then walked out to the car. Hands on my hips, I stared at the car's windshield. The threat had been so personal in the way it focused on my mom. Whoever had written it didn't know who they were dealing with. They were going down.

In the animal camera, the person had bent over as though he were tall. The Flamingo Realty video showed the person made a similar motion. I walked over and mimicked the movement, noticing that I had to stretch over a lot further to reach.

I glanced back at the garage, contemplating. Why were they trying to intimidate me? What was I getting into that was threatening them?

I returned to the house, grabbed my notebook, and took it outside to the swing. Biting my lip, I wrote a list of my discoveries. Everything from the boxes to the dog collar.

What had been so special about that collar, anyway? I closed my eyes, trying to remember it. The collar had been lying on the other side of some thick bushes. How could it have gotten there? Maybe if the dog had squeezed through the bushes? Would the collar have come off that way?

But even so, it was a dog collar. Why would they care?

I inhaled deeply, squeezing my eyes. I could picture picking it up. It was blue, with a dog tag. And there was something else. A big brown mark.

My eyes popped open. No way! Could it have been blood?

I shivered thinking I might have been driving around with Charlie Booker's blood on my dash for days without knowing.

Okay, so what was next? There'd been the boxes I'd discovered at the river. There was the shoe print I'd seen twice, once going into Charlie Booker's house, and one at my house.

I also had the clue of that creepy letter I'd received. Thinking of it made me wonder if Carlson had gotten anywhere with it. I needed to text him and find out.

Curious, I pulled the picture of the letter I'd sent to Carlson up on my phone.

Dear Stella

Everyone sees how you

Are snooping. Keep your nose clean and focus on your own

Details.

Death comes

Roaring with a vengeance

If you don't mind your own business.

Finding family far and wide,

Touching everyone loved by a snoop.

I read it twice, stopping both times at the word, details. I remember how odd it had struck me the first time I'd read it days ago. It was such an unconventional word to use in a threat letter. What type of goons were these?

Carlson had sneered when he'd read it. His words were clear

in my mind that it looked like an elementary school project, and I had to agree.

Elementary school project. Hmmm. I read it again. I didn't get more than four lines in when I excitedly grabbed for my pen. One of my favorite assignments in fifth grade were acrostic poems. I scribbled down the first letter of each sentence.

D

E

A

D

D

R

I

F

T

I KNEW EXACTLY when I'd seen that before. In the email address at the shoe store. Deaddriftnymph.

213

This was it! I was so close! I scrambled for my phone to call Carlson.

"Hollywood," he answered in his gruff way.

I blurted, "Is there any way you can get a subpoena for the security tapes at the shoe store at the mall? We have a date."

"And why is that?"

I explained about the DeadDrift Nymph.

He snorted. "Well, we had the DeadDrift from the note figured out. Like I said, very amateurish."

So he'd already known it was an acrostic poem. "Now you have a link to the dog collar with the name Nymph," I said with satisfaction.

"You keep coming to me with your ideas, but you need to have some confidence in us. It may be hard to believe, but we do know what we're doing."

"So you don't think it was the gang of thieves anymore, then?"

"No, they're definitely guilty."

"What? How could they be? All this stuff happened after they were taken into custody."

"I said they were guilty. I didn't say of what. They definitely are the gang that was hitting the box trucks. And they rolled over on Charlie Booker."

"What? Rolled over? How can they? Charlie is dead."

"He was their fence. They'd bring him the stuff, and he'd fence it over ESale and such. They'd get rid of the boxes and the stuff they didn't want by dumping it down by the creek behind the duplex. They didn't expect the water would rise and sweep the mess down river."

"No. Way." The wall of boxes in his office stuck in my mind. It made perfect sense. "So what are you going to do now? Get a subpoena to search his house?"

"What did I tell you about your need to know status?"

"Well, I have something that might interest you. I suspect there is a room built into Charlie's office. The office was smaller than what showed on the building plans, and the window was covered in a black-out curtain."

"Very interesting," he said, his tone neutral. He wasn't going to give anything away, was he?

"Well, here's my last bit. I know of some more people who knew about my mom. Maribel and her boyfriend. When I walked up to the door the other day, they were talking about it."

"How could you tell?"

"I guess those walls must be super thin because I could hear them from outside. Not to mention, she acted quite cold with every interaction I had with her. I mean, how could she even stay in the same place that her brother had been murdered?"

"She's not fooling anyone, don't worry," Carlson answered grimly.

I couldn't think of anything else to ask him. Suddenly, even more pressing on my mind was the issue of how exactly did the letter from my mother end up on my porch?

Absentmindedly, I said goodbye. Luckily, Carlson didn't question my quick change of gears and seemed happy to end the conversation himself.

I chewed my thumbnail, staring at my phone in hand. That animal camera had turned out to be much more useful than I'd ever expected. I could totally catch the person in the act of putting the envelope there!

I logged into the app and rewound the footage slowly. Nothing happened for the longest time. Then the camera caught movement, and I paused to see. It was a bird who flew up the railing and stared at the door. Was it my little buddy? I needed to get a real bird feeder out there. Smiling, I rewound it some more.

The next flash of movement made me gasp. It was Charity Valentine! I rewound to the beginning of the scene.

The Valentine Thunderbird stopped outside my driveway with Ms. Valentine driving. A moment later, Charity hopped around from the passenger the side of the car and walked over to my mailbox. She picked something up from the ground— my letter. The mailman must have accidentally dropped it. Her lips moved as she read the address. Her face glowed with joy as she scuttled up my driveway. A moment later, she knocked on the door. When there was no answer, she tucked it under the doormat and then hurried back to her car.

Wow! She must have seen it on their way to Truly's house. If she hadn't rescued it, the letter might have blown away, and then I would have never known what my mom really thought. My heart swelled with thankfulness at Charity's selfless act.

Ms. Valentine too. As stiff as she was with me, she *did* stop and allow her sister out. I truly owed them both.

Friendships sometimes came from the most surprising places. I guess my family was getting bigger after all.

23

Despite all my good feelings during the day, things fell apart that night. I had no idea why thoughts and emotions that never would occur to me during the daylight suddenly crept out like ghoulies from the dark corners of my subconscious after the sun went down.

I could barely sleep as my imagination played with every creak the house emitted, giving me visions of creepers tip-toeing up the stairs. I felt under the pillow for a wrench I had hidden there... a tool I'd used earlier to tighten a leaky faucet.

Sighing, I gave up and turned on the lamp on my nightstand. To try and distract myself, I rifled through the rose carved box for another one of my great great grandma's letters. Wiktoria was Oscar's grandma who had escaped encroaching troops in

World War II. She'd immigrated to America to start a new life, and these letters were her correspondence with her mom back in Poland.

Unfortunately, the letters needed translating, so it had been slow work. But with a translation app, I'd been slowly able to piece together her precious history. Since it had been dad and me for so long, any roots I could find to ancestors were more priceless than I could express, as if they were threads underlining I was meant to be here, I existed. I wasn't a waif who came from nowhere.

Dearest Momma,

It's been so hard living a life here without you by my side. I look forward to the day when we are reunited. Life is going well. Remember the young baker I told you about? The one who gives me day-old bread as a gift? He has asked me out several times now. We walk along the lake in the center of the city's park and sometimes feed the ducks. His name is Thomas O'Neil, and he is such a gentleman. He makes my heart laugh, Momma, the way you once told me Papa did for you. I wish you could meet him. Maybe someday soon.

I sighed and set the letter down. I knew from Oscar that Wiktoria didn't get to see her again until years later, shortly before her mom's death. The longing to be reunited with a mom was new to me. I'd never even considered it as an option before. Yet, ever since Uncle Chris's confession, it was slowly becoming a reality.

One thing I didn't understand though. If my mom wanted to see me, why did she deny my attempt to visit? That was so hurtful, it almost crushed me.

I packed up the letter and turned out the light. I'd think about it tomorrow. As I closed my eyes, my hand slid under the pillow and grabbed the wrench.

I WOKE UP FROM A DREAM, one of those weird ones where everything feels so real, yet even in the midst of it, you know something is really off. As I lay there blinking, I couldn't help but smile. It was off all right. Even as it was fading, the memory of me being the hooting-tooting sheriff of a town still lingered.

Sunlight spilled through the window and landed in a warm square on my leg. I rolled over and checked my phone. Excitement threaded through me as I read an email requesting a showing by a potential buyer for later in the day. Yes! I was back in business!

I hurried to the bathroom for my morning routine. It was as I was in the shower that a thought hit me in mid-shampoo.

Maribel's boyfriend was not tall.

In fact, he wasn't that much taller than myself. It might not seem like much, but that thought derailed my entire momentum. I groaned and rinsed my hair.

Him not being tall meant he wasn't the guy in either of the videos. It also meant he hadn't been the one to leave the track by my mailbox. It wasn't his shoe prints that I saw leading up to Charlie Booker's house. It obviously wasn't Maribel, and the gang of thieves had already been ruled out. Which left only one obvious conclusion.

There was a third suspect involved. One I'd never considered.

But who?

More importantly, would I annoy Carlson if I talked to him about it?

I toweled dried my hair and combed out the snarls. After considering it for a moment more, I jetted off a text to Carlson. **—The person in both surveillance video's was tall. Maribel and her boyfriend aren't.**

I wonder what he'd have to say about that.

I ate breakfast (some leftover lemon cookies Mrs. Crawford had left and coffee) and scattered more seed outside for the birds. I had an hour left before my appointment, so I searched up directions on how to build a bird feeder and jotted down a list of supplies while watching my little friend gather up his meal outside.

My phone rang. I grabbed it, expecting it was Carlson with a response to my text.

It was an unknown number.

Apprehension filled me. I couldn't hide my tenseness in my greeting. "Hello?"

"Is Stella O'Neil available?"

No way was I going to give out that information, especially after all the craziness that had happened. "Who's asking?"

"This is attorney Clarence's Brighton's office. Do you know if she's available?"

I swallowed hard. "This is she."

"One moment please." There was a click and a pause. What was going on now? Had my dad gotten a lawyer involved for some reason?

The line clicked again, and a man spoke, his voice rich in timbre. "Stella O'Neil?"

"Yes."

"I'm Attorney Clarence Brighton. I represent your mother."

I flopped into the kitchen chair like a pile of falling bricks. "Yes," I whispered.

"It's come to my attention that you've been in contact with her. And apparently, you tried to visit her?"

"Yes, that's right."

"Well, I'm here to tell you that your mother was extremely disappointed to miss your visit. Hopefully, I can smooth the path to make it easier for the next time."

"What happened?"

"What happened, Ms. O'Neil, was a juxtaposition of justice that your mother has suffered from since the first day of her arrest. There's corruption and scapegoating that we've been dealing with ever since Mr. O'Neil hired me. That was partly the reason Vanessa was not allowed to visit you the other day. However, things are coming to a head and I strongly feel there will be vindication for her shortly. In the meantime, it's extremely helpful that you are back in this state. It will help at the parole meeting that she has a child here who's had no prior issues with the law." He gently coughed. "I assume that's true?"

"Yes, that's true." No trouble with the law if I didn't count the endless times I'd driven Carlson crazy.

The conversation ended with him asking for my email. He

said he would set up another time for me to visit my mother if I was still agreeable. Of course, I agreed, although I have to admit, even after her letter, there was some trepidation.

We hung up. I hadn't a chance to put the phone down when it rang again. It still was not Carlson. This time it was Kari.

24

*K*ari's didn't bother with a greeting. "Stella, you're never going to believe it, but we have another listing."

I heard her statement, however, I was thinking about something else. Kari didn't sound like her usual peppy self. She sounded like she was trying to fake enthusiasm.

"Kari, you feeling okay?"

"What? Yes, of course. Now, are you going to ask me where the new listing is?"

"Tell me. Where is it?"

"It's with the Lincoln's." There was a dramatic pause. "The neighbor's of Charlie Booker."

"Whaaat?" Yeah, I dragged out the what. The coincidence was startling.

"Seriously. And I'm passing it over to you, champ."

"You are? Why?" That was weird. Usually, real estate agents wanted to hang on to their clients. Was she really sick? What was going on?

Before I could form the questions, she said succinctly, "Joe and I just got an April fool's surprise. Only it wasn't a joke."

Huh? Wait... was she saying...

"Yeah, yeah, yeah. I'm pregnant. Before you kid around like my father-in-law just did and ask if we know what caused this, all I can say is that Joe and I use the same soap." She cleared her throat. "Showers are dangerous for us."

"Wha—uh. Congratulations!" I said, drumming up as much enthusiasm as I could in the midst of my surprise.

"Thanks. I already feel like the size of a house. Although it didn't help when my sister-in-law told me I was huge and asked if I wasn't sure it was twins."

"Oh, my gosh! You are so not huge! I would have never guessed. In fact, I'm still in shock."

She laughed. "I zinged her back. I just told her that yes, I was getting bigger, and I was hoping she could loan me some of her clothes in a few months."

I snorted. "Good for you."

"It's a shock, but we're getting kind of excited ourselves. I secretly always hoped for three kids, so this is good all around. Anyway, with this horrid morning sickness, I'm going to be taking it easy for a bit. So that means you get the new prospects."

Which meant money. "Well, great!"

"Hopefully, I'll feel better soon. I heard there's a girl's night out scheduled? You've met my friend, Georgie?"

"I did! She's my grandpa's neighbor. I could always use some new friends."

"She's one in a million. And the more I get to know you, I'm considering you the same way."

Aww. That was incredibly sweet. I said as much and then we hung up. I smiled as I got ready for work. The family kept getting bigger. And I was learning more and more that family wasn't necessarily blood.

On my way to the Flamingo Realty, my long anticipated phone call came. I answered on my car's audio. "Hello?"

"Stella, it's Carlson. You have a minute?"

"Yes, I absolutely do. And I have a few things—"

"I've got something to share that I probably shouldn't," he interrupted. Well, that spiked my interest. I let him win the interruption death-match.

"It's Maribel. I hate to disappoint you because I know you had your heart set on this, but both her and her boyfriend have an alibi at the time of Charlie's murder."

"What?"

He heaved a sigh. "You made some good points about the shoe size, so you should be pleased. They both check out as being at a mini golf course, tickets, scorecards, and all."

"You're serious?"

"Yeah, so our hunt for a suspect is still on. By the way, if you share that with anyone, I will emphatically deny it."

"I would never," I swore. We said goodbye.

So I was right. I tallied up the details I knew for sure. The guy was tall. He knew me. He knew where I lived, and he knew that I had the dog collar. He knew about my mother. He was married, and he wore a health watch on his wrist.

228

If he knew me, that meant I knew him as well. *Think, Stella, think.*

Kari wasn't at the realty office when I arrived, but I honestly hadn't expected her after our little phone call.

I sat at my desk and read the listing information she'd told me about. William and Marge Lincoln, duplex B. I already knew what to expect from Charlie's place, and there were no surprises. Two bedrooms and an office. I was curious what their office would look like, in comparison to Charlie's. I also remembered how Marge had said that people came in and out of Charlie's place. I wonder if they ever knew or even suspected that illegal things were going on next door.

Excitement churned inside me as I printed up the contract. While it zipped through the machine, I put a phone call in to them.

"Mr. Lincoln," I said when a man answered.

"Yes?"

"I'm Stella O'Neil. I represent Flamingo Realty."

The pause on the other end lasted long enough that I needed to check my cell phone to see if we were still connected. "Hello?" I asked.

"Sorry, yes, okay. So you have papers for us to sign?"

"That's right. I have that along with some comps to go over to show you what I think your place is worth. Are you free today?"

"Yes, absolutely."

"Wonderful! In about an hour?"

He agreed, and I hung up. I had a few things to finish before I was ready to leave.

About forty minutes later, I'd gathered my paperwork, finished my comps, came up with a showing folder, and I was ready to go. Before I left, however, I hovered outside Uncle Chris's office.

"Stella." He glanced up, his eyes eager although the creases between his brows made him look stressed. "How are you?"

I hung on to the door handle. "Can I come in for a minute?"

"Yes! Of course! Absolutely!" He jerked forward as if he were going to stand before relaxing and pointing to a chair.

I sank into the seat. The air was thick with... what was it? Fear, maybe. I couldn't tell from which one of us the emotion was coming from.

"So, if I can start," I said quietly.

He nodded and patted his pocket where he normally kept his

cigar. It was a tell he had when he was especially uncomfortable.

"I understand that you were caught in a trap that my dad put into place when we moved to Seattle. Because my dad never told me about my mom, you never had permission to tell your part."

His lips opened a fraction, and it seemed like he was holding his breath.

"Guilt must have consumed you ever since I've moved out here. You heard my questions asking why you were so distant from your dad, Oscar. And you were muzzled to tell me the real reason."

Oh, man. I swear his eyes appeared misty now. I swallowed and continued. "I spoke with Grandpa, and he gave me his version of the events. I think it would be very helpful for you to meet him for some coffee and hear his side of it. I know there are some details about the whole event that might surprise you."

He rubbed his great hand down his face. "It was an awful night, Stella. I can't ever tell you how sorry I am. You see, I parked in front of my dealer's house and your mom was supposed to run in and get some stuff for me. I didn't think it would be a big deal. I was so so stupid."

"Was my mom addicted?"

He stared at me. "I think once you're addicted, you're always addicted. But she beat it. She was clean and happy. She loved her family. She loved you. It was all my fault. I dragged her back in one night, begging her for a favor. It's something that I'll never forgive myself for."

He stared down at the desk. A circle of a tear droplet splashed on its surface. "I'm so sorry, Stella. The guilt has eaten me up. I've robbed you and Steve of a family. It's one of the reasons why I've never searched for a family of my own. I know I didn't deserve one."

Those final details fell into place. My mom wasn't actively using drugs at the time. She loved me. She'd truly been in the wrong place at the wrong time. There were still some pieces missing, but there was enough there to satisfy me. What mattered now were the wrinkles of grief on Uncle Chris's face that echoed the ones in the cheap suit he was wearing. This was a man who'd spent his life punishing himself.

Enough was enough.

"Uncle Chris, I love you. I forgive you. Let's figure this out."

He stared at me, his lips pressed together. I stood up and walked over. He did the same, his chair roughly knocking into the wall as he got to his feet. I reached him and he hugged me.

"I have one request," I gasped, squeezed in a bear hug.

"What's that?"

"I mean it. Let's meet with Oscar and do this as a family."

He didn't answer. Had I asked too much? Then I felt him nod. The nod shuddered right through his body. "Okay, Stella. Let's do it."

25

After the hug and a few back pats, I left Uncle Chris's office, already a little late for my appointment. He promised to make good on his end of the deal to contact Oscar.

I predicted a spaghetti dinner in our future.

Rushing a bit, I carried the folder to the car and headed one more time for Charlie Booker's place.

I had to admit, it was creepy to drive to the same address, albeit down a different driveway. I parked and got out. William Lincoln met me at the door.

It was hard not to smile at seeing him. The tall man wore tiny shorts with skinny legs poking out like a flamingo's. He carried the same tropical theme in his overly-large Hawaiian shirt.

His wife was dressed much more conservatively. She wore blue jeans and a striped sweater. She did like the makeup though, as her blue eyeshadow demonstrated.

They ushered me in and I walked through the house as Lincoln and his wife followed. The house was clean and smelled like fresh paint, but there were still a few things they needed to address before I came back in the morning to take photo's for the listing. Simple things like cleaning the vents in the bathroom and dusting the molding.

Marge led me into the office, which I confess, I'd been dying to see. Especially since I suspected Charlie had built a closet over on his side.

Sure enough, their room was nearly twice as big. The extra space just made sense. I wondered why it hadn't stood out to me more at Charlie's place.

There was a table under the window filled with hooks, bits of bright yarns, beads, and feathers.

"I sell fly-fishing lures online," William said, when he caught me studying them.

"Wow! Do you like to fish?"

"I do some fly-fishing. She doesn't," he answered with a jerk of his thumb in his wife's direction.

Marge shrugged. "I have different hobbies. I like to sew and knit."

There was a huge quilt hanging on the wall. "Did you make this?" I asked.

She shook her head no, with a smile. "My grandma did. That's the wedding ring pattern. She gave it to us when we got married."

"It's lovely," I said, walked closer to examine it.

"Stella, could you come give your opinion of our back yard? Should we spruce it up with plants?" William asked.

"Yes, of course!" I turned to follow him. As I did, I heard someone laugh behind me. I spun around, startled.

"Oh, don't worry. It's just the neighbor's TV. Unfortunately, the walls are pretty thin around here," Marge said.

I wondered if that would be a problem showing this place. "That's too bad. I never heard anything when I was over there a few days ago with the buyers."

"We're pretty quiet. Unlike those blabbermouths." Marge leaned in close and whispered. "Especially that sister of his. I know I should feel sorry for her after the terrible thing that happened to Charlie, but she drives me nuts. Always banging and moving around at all hours of the night."

"I see. Is that why you're moving?" I asked.

"That's a big part of it. Lincoln's really keen to go. Especially now that poor Charlie is gone. Seems like she's put her roots in and is there to stay now."

We walked into the living room where William opened the sliding glass door. I followed him outside.

Their patio was clean with a couple chairs around an umbrella-covered table. The back fence showed a few new boards from a recent repair. There was a huge flower garden with more gnomes.

"It seems pretty good to me. Just keep it mowed." I pointed to the gnomes. "So someone's a collector."

William gave a wry smile and nodded in Marge's direction. She raised her hand, blushing. "That would be me."

I smiled. "They're super cute but maybe weed a few out in the front yard. And, if you can, add some potted plants on the porch, as well as a new coat of paint to the front door. Those things will go far in terms of curb appeal. We want those potential buyers on the hook as they walk up to the house." I mimed fishing, hoping William would appreciate the analogy.

He smirked. I wandered back inside and through the kitchen

where I pointed out a few cupboard doors that needed to be tightened up. Other than that, I could tell this home would show great. Marge was a good housekeeper and everything was neat as a pin.

William led me into the garage, his long white legs still teasing me to dare to giggle. I was proud of myself for resisting. The garage's interior had that musty scent that most garages seemed to have. It was clean as well, with boxes on the shelves, a car parked on one side, and light shining through a little dog door.

"Everything in here looks great," I said, and then followed him back to the kitchen.

"So, what do you think?" Marge asked.

"Well, if it's possible, pack as much as you can and put it in storage, or even take it out to the garage if you have to. Make this place seem as empty and as full of possibility as you can. Also, don't forget the things I suggested to do to your front porch. Last, but not least, no air fresheners, no matter how tempting they seem. They usually backfire and can even turn a potential buyer off."

I pulled out the contract and the comps and then we discussed what price they were hoping to sell the place. Not surprisingly, it was for the same amount that Charlie had once had his listed at. When we finished going over and signing the paperwork, I packed everything up and left them with the assurance that I would be back in the morning to take pictures.

As I sat outside in the car, I couldn't help thinking about how life moves forward. I glanced over at Charlie Booker's old place. How would you access the hidden space in that office? I never recalled seeing a door in the room, only a window and a bookcase and a huge pile of boxes.

I squinted hard, trying to remember the room. I remember the buyer looking around as I yanked open the black-out curtains. He'd admired the view. We'd talked about how quiet it was there, and then laughed when we heard a dog barking.

My fingers froze clenched around the steering wheel. A dog barking. In my mind's eye, I saw the dog door in the garage, and then the repair to the backyard fence.

No dog.

I swiveled to look at the end of the driveway. A thick hedge of bushes ran along the street. It was on the other side of those that I found the unbuckled dog collar.

The one with the strange brown stain.

Someone tapped on my window.

I jumped, startled.

William Lincoln chuckled. "Sorry for scaring you. I have one more question I forgot to ask you earlier."

I stared up at him, my pulse pounding. He pantomimed unrolling the window, his slim fingers only centimeters on the other side of the glass. The diamonds in his wedding ring sparkled.

I glanced at the electronic button in the door. Slowly my hand rose.

"Just one question," he repeated, smiling.

I hit the lock button. I tried my best to do it inconspicuously, but I think he noticed. The expression on his face dropped into confusion.

"I'm sorry!" I yelled. "I'm late for another showing. I'll call you!" I waved cheerily, hoping to throw him off, and then put the car in reverse. Then, staring over my shoulder, I stepped on the gas hard enough for him to jump back.

I don't know what my problem was. I'd potentially just lost a client. However, my intuition was telling me something was very off. And if there was one thing I'd learned in my life, it was to trust my gut.

Once out on the road, I laid my hand on my stomach. "What are you saying?" It was good on giving the warning flags, however, it seemed to neglect sharing the important details on why there was a warning.

Think, Stella. This can't be that hard. What bothered me at the house? I passed the hidden driveway with the neighbor that had come out to his porch with the shot gun. He'd been complaining about people running behind his house. "That's where the river is," he'd said.

Shadows from the trees streaked across the road. Boxes. Boxes. Boxes.

Charlie Booker's office, the one with the missing space. There had been that bookshelf. The black-out curtains.

My mind zipped to William Lincoln's office. The hanging quilt. The thin walls. And most importantly. No dog.

I hit the steering wheel. Why hadn't I seen all of this sooner?

My adrenaline gave me a kick in the pants. I had to call Carlson. I knew who had killed Charlie Booker.

I pulled over to the side of the road, shaking with excitement. Before I put the call through, I did a quick internet search to be sure I was on the right track.

The search results made me squeal. I *knew* it! I scrambled for my phone and hit dial.

"Hollywood? You okay?" Carlson answered.

"What do the words 'dead drift' and 'nymph' mean to you?" I blurted.

"Err, is this a joke?"

"I'm completely serious. When I say them together, do they mean anything to you?"

"Not really. Sounds like a slasher film."

I shivered. If he only knew how close to the truth he was. "They're fly-fishing terms. A nymph is one of those baby bugs that lives underwater. That's what the fisherman is trying to mimic with his casts. And dead drifting is when the fly moves with the current, like it's a dead bug."

There was a pause as he tried to process, and I realized I'd started in the middle of the conversation and needed to back up. Before I could do that, it was his turn to be excited. "Hang on. Dead Drift. Like that weird note you got."

"Yes!" I may have been louder than necessary in my excitement. Lowering my voice, I added, "And Nymph on the dog collar. Both were used in the email address."

"You've got my attention," he said.

I took a deep breath and ran down all my clues. At least, I hoped they were clues. They sure added up to me. "From my first visit to Charlie Booker's house, I noticed that the neighbor would watch me from his window. I caught him the first time because his wedding ring sparkled, catching my eye. Today I saw that it had a channel of diamonds on it."

Carlson made an encouraging noise.

"That was something that stood out in all the videos. The person was tall and he had on a sparkling ring."

243

"Hmph," Carlson grunted. "I hope there's more to it than that. A huge portion of the US are tall, married men."

"I have tons more stuff." Quickly, I reiterated that Charlie Booker was the ringleader of the box truck hijacking.

"You're good, Stella, but we already have that covered, remember?" Carlson answered. "And what does that have to do with the neighbor?"

"Well, remember how I told you that Charlie's office was a lot smaller than it should be? I wondered if it was a closet, but there had been no door. What was there was a large bookcase."

"Are you about to Scooby Doo me?"

"I totally am. I think Charlie built a partition and hid the stuff he was fencing in the space behind the secret bookcase door."

"That won't be hard to confirm with a subpoena. Keep going."

"So that day that I was showing Charlie's house, we heard a dog barking next door. I remember because we were joking that it was a quiet neighborhood. And today, while I was on Lincoln's side, I heard the TV going from Charlie's house. In Lincoln's house, the office is his work space. He makes fly fishing lures."

"Okay...."

"Well, This proves that Lincoln could hear everything that was going on in the other duplex's office area. I think Lincoln knew about the fencing, knew that Charlie had a ton of money over there. And knew about Charlie's secret room. The greed got to him. He knew about the gang of criminals that were constantly in and out of Booker's place and came up with a plan. With so many bad guys involved, he must have figured no one would ever suspect him."

"Just one problem. Charlie's door was locked, and no money was reported missing."

"Okay, so I have an answer for that. Remember how the TV was destroyed? I think when Lincoln was in there, he saw the surveillance video on the TV. In order to not make anyone look for the recordings, he smashed the TV. Then he stole the laptop to further complicate tracking anything down."

"We never saw cameras."

"Yeah, while I was over there, I never saw any cameras, either. My only clue was the divided screens on the television. I thought they might be the outlet kind."

"Okay. Still not explaining the money or locked door."

"Getting in was easy for Lincoln. He waited until Maribel and her boyfriend left, then walked up to the door and knocked. Those were his footprints I saw on the way in.

Maybe he had some neighborly excuse to chat with him, but obviously, Charlie felt comfortable letting him in."

"And getting out?"

"Like I said, he knew about the hidden room from listening on the other side of the wall. He killed Charlie Booker, destroyed the TV, snatched up the laptop and went into Charlie's office. He moved the bookshelf, where presumably the money and rest of the goods were kept."

"And then?"

"Once inside, he busted through the wall to his office. After he moved all the stuff into his place, he slid Charlie's bookshelf shut behind him. When I was at Lincoln's place today, I smelled fresh paint. There was a huge quilt hanging on the dividing office wall. When I went to examine it, Lincoln was in an awful hurry to get me out of the room with an excuse of looking at his backyard. My guess is that you look behind the quilt, you'll see a fresh patch job."

"Nice, Stella! Now what do you think about the dog collar?"

"Here's where it get's tricky, because I don't have any hard facts. My guess is that at some point after Lincoln murdered Charlie, his little dog snuck through the fresh hole in the wall. Maybe it happened when Lincoln was hauling things in and out and he didn't notice. By the time he did notice, the dog had discovered Charlie. The animal may have had blood on his collar. Maybe Lincoln didn't have time to deal with Nymph, so he shooed the dog outside into the backyard until he was finished. From there, I think the dog escaped."

"What makes you think that?"

"There were fresh boards at the back of the fence from a repair job. Between wiggling through that, and then scurrying through some brush, the dog lost its collar. I think the dog is gone for good. I didn't see it there today at the Lincoln's house."

"How did you know he had a dog?"

"Besides hearing it bark the other day, there was a dog door in the garage."

"Nicely done. I'm impressed."

"Thank you," I said humbly.

"I'll get on the horn to see about that subpoena."

"Keep me updated?"

"I'll do what I can. It's not that I don't trust you. It's that we've got rules and all."

"Of course. Well, I'll take whatever I can get."

He laughed at that. "I owe you a burger, I think."

"I'll take it!"

We were about to hang up when his frantic, "Hey, Stella," stopped me.

"What?"

"One more question. You have any idea why he targeted you with that note and stuff? I mean, how did he know about your mother?"

"It was the reason why I'd suspected Maribel for so long. You see, she had my notebook that had my mom's information in it. Remember how I said I could hear them discussing her from outside on the front porch. Well, if I could hear them, so could Lincoln. They probably talked about it a few times."

"Why would Lincoln come after you?"

"He must have seen me pick up the dog collar. Or, maybe he saw it on my car's dash the many times I was over there. I even posted about it on the town's site. He knew it could potentially be tracked back to him. Honestly, it was mostly paranoia on Lincoln's part because, had he left me alone, I never would have had the motivation to figure out how the pieces went together."

"And you think he wanted the collar because the dog had been around Charlie's body?"

"I suspect so. There was a weird brown stain on the collar. It didn't look like mud. It very well could have been dried blood."

"All right, that's enough to go on. Until I get that subpoena and figure this out, you could be in danger. Keep an eye on your surroundings and stay safe. I'm looking forward to that burger, Hollywood. Don't think you can cheat me." I could hear the smile in his voice.

I laughed. "I wouldn't dare, Carlson. Talk with you later."

*L*ater turned out to be about two days. It was at that point that the police called me to go down to the station to give an official statement. The police had located the dog collar in Lincoln's tackle box. Also in the tackle box was a very sharp scaling knife, one that had a suspicious brown stain along the handle. Lincoln tried to say it was fish blood but preliminary tests had already proved it to be human. Detectives were still waiting on the official DNA results, however, there was another clue that cinched the case. Discovered in one of the boxes inside the garage was a stack of magazines with various letters cut out from them. Letters that matched the threatening message I'd received.

William Lincoln was arrested for the murder of Charlie

Booker. His wife maintained she knew nothing. As far as I knew, she was still under investigation.

Right now, I was talking on the phone with Attorney Clarence Brighton while watching through the window with some admiration as Richie set up a security system.

Richie had insisted his heart couldn't take seeing cop cars at my house anymore and the animal cam wasn't cutting it. Even though I'd tried to reassure him that I was fine, he still bought one of those doorbell cameras along with a perimeter alarm.

He made me smile, making me mishear the last thing that Attorney Brighton said. "What was that?" I asked.

"I was saying, things are looking up. I'll be in touch again soon."

"All right, thank you. I'm looking forward to it." We said goodbye, and I walked into the kitchen for some iced tea. Moments later, I carried two glasses to the front porch.

A few intimidating wires stuck out from the wall of the house like cat whiskers. Richie held a pair of wire strippers. "Hey, you. Good conversation?" He reached up to take the tea. "Thanks!"

"Pretty good, I guess. It was my mom's lawyer."

"And?" He took a sip and then tucked a wire fastener in his

mouth while stripping the wires. Satisfied, he twisted the fastener on them, binding them together. He started to screw them under the back of the doorbell.

I sighed. "He says I'm definitely cleared to be one of my mom's visitors. He scheduled a visiting day for me tomorrow. But after the disaster I went through last time... I'm just not sure. I wanted him to go with me but I don't have the money."

"Money?"

"Yeah. He's one of those weirdos who likes to be paid to work and appear." I gave a satirical grin.

He grinned. "How is he being paid now?"

"My Grandpa pays him."

Things were silent for a while as he finished screwing the box to the wall. I could feel he was thinking deeply.

"So you're worried about going alone?" he finally asked.

I nodded. For some reason the space between us seemed to close.

Richie replaced his tools back into his bag and slowly stood up. I caught the clean scent of soap or aftershave. "You don't have to be alone."

My mouth suddenly was dry.

He stared at me, eyes dark and serious. "I've been waiting. I know you've been through a lot, so I've been taking my time, letting you lead the way. But you have to know, I'm standing right here."

A thrill of excitement ran through my body. I wanted to smile, laugh, even to jump in his arms, I swear I did.

I hesitated.

That hesitation was brought on by a kaleidoscope tumbling through me in sharp colors of fear. I'd just gone through a yo-yo of emotions with my mom and family betrayals.

Could I turn that fear off? Could I be vulnerable again?

I felt it then—a need. A longing to be close to someone, to have someone say that everything was going to be okay... that I was okay. My heart was crying out for someone to hold my hand when I went to see my mom tomorrow.

I didn't want to be alone anymore.

He leaned in close. His breath tickled my cheek and promised an intimacy of a deeper, softer kind. My head turned toward his, craving it.

His fingers reached out and slowly traced up my jaw line until they threaded through my hair. I felt the strength of his body, so close, so warm. I wanted to relax and be encompassed by his arms. Held against his broad chest, chin tipped up. Kissed.

My breath came in tiny shallow sips. We waited, His fingers gently stroking through my hair, his pulse jumping in his throat, his whiskered chin held *just there*. Waiting to capture my mouth. Waiting for my signal.

The seconds seemed to last for eternity. I breathed out as Carlson came to mind.

Finally, I turned my head down. No. I couldn't do this. I couldn't do it until I knew it was the right thing for the both of us. That it wasn't me just using someone to fill a need in my life.

I stared back up sadly, and his eyes mirrored mine. He was so good, so handsome. "I'm sorry," I whispered.

"You have nothing to be sorry for. Like I told you, I'm a patient man. Besides, I have a theory."

"A theory?"

He nodded. "Yeah. You see, when I was a teenager, my dad always told me to find a woman who was also my best friend. He said he had that with my mom. "It's the laughter that gets you through, son." Of course, he mentioned the kisses were pretty good too."

I laughed now.

"How about you come with me to the car show. They're having a hot rod exhibition next weekend. Maybe we'll see a Super Bee."

I nodded as the space between us turned easy-going. "That sounds like a lot of fun."

He grinned. "And if you want company when you go visit your mom, I'd love to come. No strings attached."

"Thanks, Richie. That means a lot. Let me think about it."

We spent some time with him explaining how the security camera worked, and me getting acquainted with the new app. Then, after finishing the rest of his iced tea, he tipped his cowboy hat at me. "Time for me to get home and check on Ma."

"Have a good day, Richie. Thank you again for everything."

He threw the bag into the passenger seat and turned back to smile at me. Then he drove home, leaving a cloud of dust.

My heart squeezed as I watched him go. Life was so weird and complicated, wasn't it? I sighed and headed for the garage. There was something I'd been wanting to do for a while, and this was as good of a time as any.

A couple hours later, after countless YouTube videos, I had all of the pieces cut and mostly assembled. It was a bird feeder, and it was looking pretty good, if you didn't mind a little lopsidedness along the roof line. I was nailing on the last piece when a car turned into my driveway.

I glanced at it, nervous because it was unfamiliar. *Now what?*

My heart jumped into my throat as the car's door opened and the driver got out.

Dad.

Never in a million years would I have expected to see him here in Pennsylvania. He'd sworn that he'd never return and had only just started to warm up to the idea that it might be a distant possibility before the big blow up had happened.

Yet, here he was now, walking toward me.

The first thing I noticed was how thin and depressed he looked. It made me worry. I wanted my dad around for a long, long time, and not as a man who was sad and missing my mom. Instead, as a man who was happy and living life.

Then I noticed how welcoming he looked. My dad. The person I loved more than anyone else in the world. I ran over and gave him a hug, the hug I'd needed all along.

"Stella!" he said, capturing me in his arms. He kissed the top of my head and murmured, "My baby girl. It's so good to see you."

256

"Dad, I can't believe you're here. I'm so glad!" I cried happy tears. Every bit of anger I felt melted away.

"Honey, I am so sorry for the way things turned out. I made so many mistakes, but I'm here now to make things right again, if you'll let me."

I sniffled and looked up at him. He was teary as well. "How are you going to do that?" I asked. I didn't doubt him. I wanted to hear his plan.

"I've been talking with.... Oscar. With my dad."

I reeled back and grabbed his jacket sleeve for support. "What?" I gasped.

"I've had to. Thinking I was losing you after all the mistakes I'd made. I had to figure it out."

"You and Oscar are okay?"

He grimaced. "I wouldn't say okay. I'd say I'm open to meeting with him. And I'd like you to be there."

"Yes! Of course, I will be!"

"He told me the lawyer has been in contact with you. The one for your mom? That there is a meeting planned between you two soon."

I nodded, hardly able to wrap my mind around the fact that my dad was standing here. In my driveway. Flesh and blood.

talk."

Waly happening?

He took my pause as a no. "It's totally fine, Stella. I get if you need to do it alone. I wanted to be available however I can support you. There's a lot of new things I'm learning as well. When your mom left that night, and I found out she'd been with your Uncle and drugs were involved, I assumed the worst. I ran. And in doing so, I never learned the truth. I ended up hurting everyone."

He took a deep breath. "You see, I made a mistake, one that I've kept making over and over again. When people hurt me deeply, I've cut them off. It was the only way I knew how to deal with the pain. The cost was higher than I realized. Even worse, you had to pay the highest price. I'm so sorry. Please forgive me."

I gulped. "It's okay, Dad. We'll figure this out."

"That's what I want. Even to the point of at least giving Oscar a chance to have his say. I want to correct my past mistakes. And my biggest reason is so that you don't ever copy that same pattern."

That made me think. Did I cut people off when I was hurt? Well, maybe temporarily, but I was already back on track with Oscar and Uncle Chris. There was, however, something

258

else that I did, a protection technique. I kept people at arm's length. I was afraid to get close, to care about someone else.

I'd have to look at that more deeply in the future. Right now, I had my dad here. We had a lot to talk about.

I could see there was a lot of repairing and family visits in our future. Between Uncle Chris, Dad and Oscar. And especially my mom. I couldn't wait to see her. And I couldn't wait to see what happened when my parents saw each other again.

As we walked into the house together, I'd thought back to when I'd first moved here. When I met Oscar, it felt like this was my last chance to bring all the men in my family back together again.

After everything blew up, I'd lost all hope in any reconciliation between them. Those men hadn't done it in all those years. I knew it would never happen, now.

Yet here it was, with these same men making all those phone calls, and now my dad flying out here. They were coming together on their own for my sake.

I realized that my falling apart was the catalyst to bring this family back together because they wanted to make it right for me. In the end, I guess that was what family was all about, after all—being there for you at your worst moments.

When I was growing up, I'd thought I was destined for great

things. Then I had years of fear that I wouldn't succeed at anything. Now I knew. If I could achieve love and have my family, then I had everything.

And right now, that was looking pretty good to me.

It was at that moment my phone blew up with a text. I fished it out to see it was from Carlson. Very uncharacteristically, he'd written all in caps. **—I JUST LEARNED SOMETHING ABOUT YOUR MOM. DON'T GO!**

The End

THANK you for reading Duplex Double Trouble. The story concludes in MidCentury Modern Murder Flamingo Mystery.

Here are a few more series to whet your appetite!

Baker Street Mysteries— Where Oscar and Kari are first introduced! Join Georgie, amateur sleuth and historical tour guide on her spooky, crazy adventures. As a fun bonus there's free recipes included!

Cherry Pie or Die

Cookies and Scream

Crème Brûlée or Slay

Drizzle of Death

Slash in the Pan

Oceanside Hotel Cozy Mysteries—Maisie runs a 5 star hotel and thought she'd seen everything. Little did she know. From haunted pirate tales to Hollywood red carpet events, she has a lot to keep her busy.

Booked For Murder

Deadly Reservation

Final Check Out

Fatal Vacancy

Suite Casualty

Angel Lake Cozy Mysteries—Elise comes home to her home town to lick her wounds after a nasty divorce. Together, with her best friend Lavina, they cook up some crazy mysteries.

The Sweet Taste of Murder

The Bitter Taste of Betrayal

The Sour Taste of Suspicion

The Honeyed Taste of Deception

The Tempting Taste of Danger

The Frosty Taste of Scandal

And here is Circus Cozy Mysteries— Meet Trixie, the World's Smallest Lady Godiva. She may be small but she's learning she has a lion's heart.

Cirque de Slay

Big Top Treachery